感恩劉毅老師，感謝「一口氣英語」！

　　我們從幼兒園學英語，學到高中、大學，甚至博士畢業，會做很多試卷，可是一見到外國人，往往張口結舌，聽不懂，不會說，變成英語上的「聾啞人」！「聾啞英語」如同癌症，困擾了數代英語人！我們多希望有一種教材，有一種方法，有一種良丹妙藥，讓我們治癒「聾啞英語」頑症，同時又能兼顧考試。直到遇見台灣「英語天王」劉毅老師的「一口氣英語」。

劉毅老師頒發授權書
給趙艷花校長

趙老師學校主辦，劉毅老師親授「一口氣英語萬人講座」

　　「劉毅英文」稱雄台灣補教界近半個世紀，「一口氣英語」功不可沒！劉毅老師前無古人，後無來者的英語功底，成就了「一口氣英語」的靈魂。「一口氣英語」從詞彙學到文法，從演講到作文，從中英文成語到會話，各種題材、各種形式，包羅萬象。

康克教育感恩劉毅老師

感恩劉毅老師發明「一口氣英語」，2014年5月河南省鄭州市「康克教育」孫參軍老師，在接受「一口氣英語會話、演講」師訓後，經授權迅速在中原四省——河南省、河北省、安徽省、山西省，20多個城市、30多個分校開班授課，人數由5,000人倍速增長至12,000人次。

孫參軍校長與劉毅老師

2016年11、12月，受邀到「中國少林功夫弟子武僧院」，推廣「一口氣英語」教學，實現500人大班授課，全場武僧將少林功夫與「一口氣英語」完美詮釋，為打造未來功夫明星堅實的語言功底。

贏在學習‧勝在改變

　　福建省福州市「沖聰教育」劉偉老師接受「一口氣英語演講」師訓後，讓同學從害怕、緊張、不敢，到充滿自信，並勇敢參加第十三屆「星星火炬英語風采大賽」，32位學生於福建省賽中，取得優異的成績。評委表示，學生演講的內容很有深度，驚訝不已！同年「沖聰教育」學生人數快速激增！

「一飛教育」陳佳明校長主持，
由劉毅老師親授「一口氣英語全國師資培訓」

劉毅獲頒「中國教育聯盟終身成就獎」

牛新哲主席代表「中國教育培訓聯盟」感謝「一口氣英語」創始人劉毅老師，終身致力於英語教育之卓越成就，給與全方位的獎勵，奠定角色模範，繼而鼓勵後輩，投入更多心力於英語教育領域，特別頒發「中國教育聯盟終生成就獎」，劉毅老師成為首位獲此殊榮的台灣之光。

劉毅老師於2017年2月6日在台北舉行「用會話背7000字」講座

初級英語檢定複試測驗①詳解

寫作能力測驗詳解

第一部份：單句寫作

第 1~5 題：句子改寫

1. Swimming in the river is dangerous.

It's ＿＿＿＿＿＿＿＿＿＿＿＿＿＿＿＿＿＿＿＿＿.

　　重點結構：以 It 為虛主詞引導的句子

　　解　　答：It's dangerous to swim in the river.

　　句型分析：It's + 形容詞 + to V.

　　説　　明：虛主詞 it 代替不定詞片語，不定詞片語則擺在句
　　　　　　　尾，故 swimming in the river 改為 to swim in
　　　　　　　the river。

　　* swim〔swɪm〕*v.* 游泳　　river〔'rɪvə〕*n.* 河
　　dangerous〔'dendʒərəs〕*adj.* 危險的

2. I got someone to mail the letter yesterday.

I had ＿＿＿＿＿＿＿＿＿＿＿＿＿＿＿＿＿＿＿＿＿.

　　重點結構：「have + *sb.* + 原形動詞」的用法

　　解　　答：I had someone mail the letter yesterday.

　　句型分析：主詞 + have + 受詞 + 原形動詞

　　説　　明：「get + *sb.* + to V.」表「叫某人做～」，若用
　　　　　　　使役動詞 have，接受詞後，須用原形動詞。

　　* mail〔mel〕*v.* 郵寄　　letter〔'lɛtə〕*n.* 信

3. You enjoy roller-skating, and he does, too.

Not only _____.

重點結構：「not only…but also~」的用法

解　答：Not only you but also he enjoys roller-skating.

句型分析：Not only + A + but also + B + 動詞

説　明：「not only A but also B」表「不但 A，而且 B」，
做主詞時，動詞的單複數視 B 來決定，因為此片語
的強調部份是 B。這裡的 he 是第三人稱單數，故動
詞用 enjoys。

＊ enjoy〔ɪnˋdʒɔɪ〕v. 喜歡
roller-skate〔ˋrolɚˌsket〕v. 輪式溜冰

4. Every time she comes, she must bring a present to us.

She never comes _____.

重點結構：「never + 一般動詞 + without + 動名詞」的用法

解　答：She never comes without bringing a present to
us.

句型分析：主詞 + never + 動詞 + without + 動名詞

説　明：按句意，「每當她來訪時，她一定帶禮物給我們。」
這題若用 never（絕不）表示否定的句意，又接
without（沒有），為雙重否定，表「每…必~」。
without 為介系詞，後面須接動名詞。

＊ *every time* 每當　　present〔ˋprɛzn̩t〕n. 禮物

5. Where is the nearest police station?

Tell me _____.

重點結構：間接問句做名詞子句

　解　答：<u>Tell me where the nearest police station is.</u>

句型分析：Tell me + where + 主詞 + 動詞

　説　明：在 wh- 問句前加 Tell me，形成間接問句，必須把 be 動詞 is 放在最後面，並把問號改成句點。

* *police station* 警察局

第 6～10 題：句子合併

6. My father painted the house.
   I helped my father.

   _____.

　重點結構：「help + *sb.* + (to) V.」的用法

　解　答：<u>I helped my father (to) paint the house.</u>

句型分析：help + 受詞 + 原形動詞或不定詞

　説　明：句意是「我幫爸爸油漆房子」，用動詞 help 造句，help 之後所接的不定詞的 to 可省略。

* paint〔pent〕*v.* 油漆

7. I'm talking about that stranger.
   That stranger is wearing a red sweater.（用 in 合併）

   _____.

　重點結構：in 的用法

　解　答：<u>I'm talking about that stranger in a red sweater.</u>

句型分析：名詞 + in + 衣服

説　明：wearing a red sweater 可改成 in a red sweater，
修飾 that stranger。

* **talk about** 談論　　stranger〔'strendʒɚ〕n. 陌生人
sweater〔'swɛtɚ〕n. 毛衣

8. Mr. Lin invited the woman.
The woman is not very tall. (用 who 合併)

_____.

重點結構：由 who 引導的形容詞子句
解　答：<u>Mr. Lin invited the woman who is not very tall.</u>
句型分析：Mr. Lin invited the woman + who + 動詞
説　明：句意是「林先生邀請那位長得不是很高的女士」，
在合併兩句時，用 who 代替先行詞 the woman，
引導形容詞子句，在子句中做主詞。

* invite〔ɪn'vaɪt〕v. 邀請

9. Linda looks very funny.
Linda wears that cowboy hat. (用 if 合併)

_____.

重點結構：由連接詞 if 引導的副詞子句
解　答：<u>Linda looks very funny if she wears that
cowboy hat.</u>
句型分析：Linda looks very funny + if + 主詞 + 動詞
説　明：按照句意，「琳達如果戴上那頂牛仔帽，會看起來
很好笑」。用連接詞 if 連接兩句時，if 要引導完整
的子句，即「if + 主詞 + 動詞」。

* funny〔ˈfʌnɪ〕*adj.* 好笑的　　***cowboy hat*** 牛仔帽

10. Miss White moved the heavy box.
No one helped her with it.（用反身代名詞合併）

_____.

重點結構：「by + 反身代名詞」的用法

解　答：Miss White moved the heavy box by herself.

句型分析：主詞 + 動詞 + 受詞 + by + 反身代名詞

說　明：由 No one helped her with it. 可知「懷特小姐
自己一個人搬運很重的箱子」，用片語「by
oneself」，表「獨力；靠自己」，Miss White
為女性第三人稱單數，故反身代名詞用 herself。

* move〔muv〕*v.* 移動；搬動

第 11～15 題：重組

11. Ronald's _____.
been / away / several times / has / car / towed

重點結構：現在完成式字序及被動語態字序

解　答：Ronald's car has been towed away several
times.

句型分析：主詞 + have/has + been + 過去分詞

說　明：一般現在完成式的結構是「主詞 + have/has + 過
去分詞」，而一般被動語態的結構是「主詞 + be
動詞 + 過去分詞」，be 動詞的現在完成式是
have/has been，故形成此句。

* ***tow away*** 拖吊　　several〔'sɛvərəl〕*adj.* 好幾個

12. It's ＿＿＿＿＿＿＿＿＿＿＿＿＿＿＿＿＿＿＿＿.

others / wrong / copy / your answers / to let

重點結構：以 It 爲虛主詞引導的句子

解　答：It's wrong to let others copy your answers.

句型分析：It's ＋ 形容詞 ＋ to V.

説　明：先找出形容詞 wrong 之後，找出不定詞 to let，
又 let 爲使役動詞，接受詞後，須接原形動詞。

* wrong〔rɔŋ〕*adj.* 不對的　　copy〔'kɑpɪ〕*v.* 抄寫

13. Judy ＿＿＿＿＿＿＿＿＿＿＿＿＿＿＿＿＿＿.

to / be / too / is / on the school / short / basketball team

重點結構：「too ＋ 形容詞 ＋ to V.」的用法

解　答：Judy is too short to be on the school basketball
team.

句型分析：主詞 ＋ be 動詞 ＋ too ＋ 形容詞 ＋ to V.

説　明：這題的意思是說「茱蒂長得太矮，不能參加籃球
校隊」，用「too…to V.」合併兩句，表「太…
而不能～」。

* team〔tim〕*n.* 隊

14. The question ＿＿＿＿＿＿＿＿＿＿＿＿＿＿＿＿.

children / answer it / that / is / hard / can't / so

重點結構：「so ＋ 形容詞 ＋ that 子句」的用法

解　答：<u>The question is so hard that children can't answer it.</u>

句型分析：主詞 + be 動詞 + so + 形容詞 + that + 主詞 + 動詞

說　明：這題的意思是說「這問題太難了，所以小孩答不出來」，合併兩句時，用「so…that~」，表「如此…以致於~」。

*　hard〔hɑrd〕adj. 困難的

15. People _____.
water / might / their health / afraid / that / are / harm / pollution

重點結構：「be 動詞 + afraid + that + 主詞 + 動詞」的用法

解　答：<u>People are afraid that water pollution might harm their health.</u>

句型分析：主詞 + be 動詞 + afraid + that + 主詞 + 動詞

說　明：afraid（害怕的）的用法為：

$\begin{cases} \text{be 動詞 + afraid of + N / V-ing} \\ \text{be 動詞 + afraid + that + 主詞 + 動詞} \end{cases}$

*　pollution〔pəˈluʃən〕n. 污染
　　harm〔hɑrm〕v. 傷害　　health〔hɛlθ〕n. 健康

第二部份：段落寫作

題目：這是妳／你一天的生活。請根據以下的圖片寫一篇約 50 字的
短文。

I usually get up *around six o'clock*. I start my day by brushing my teeth and washing my face. *Then* I have my breakfast before going to school. I arrive at school at seven thirty. At school, I have a lot of classes, like math, science, and English. I come home *at four o'clock*. After dinner, I do my homework. *When it's nine o'clock*, I go to bed and hope that I have a sweet dream.

　　我通常大約六點起床。我以刷牙和洗臉開始我的一天。然後我在去上學前吃早餐。我在 7 點 30 分到學校。在學校的時候，我有很多課程，像是數學、科學，和英語。我在四點回到家。晚餐後，我做功課。9 點的時候，我上床睡覺，並希望有個美夢。

get up 起床　　around〔əˋraʊnd〕*adv.* 大約
teeth〔tiθ〕*n. pl.* 牙齒
brush〔brʌʃ〕*v.* 刷　　face〔fes〕*n.* 臉
have〔hæv〕*v.* 吃　　arrive〔əˋraɪv〕*v.* 到達
a lot of 很多　　class〔klæs〕*n.* 課
science〔ˋsaɪəns〕*n.* 自然科學　　hope〔hop〕*v.* 希望
sweet〔swit〕*adj.* 甜美的　　dream〔drim〕*n.* 夢

口說能力測驗詳解

*請在 15 秒內完成並唸出下列自我介紹的句子:

My seat number is （複試座位號碼後 5 碼）, and my test number is （初試准考證號碼後 5 碼）.

I. 複誦

共五題。題目不印在試卷上,由耳機播出,每題播出兩次,兩次之間大約有一至二秒的間隔。聽完兩次後,請馬上複誦一次。

1. What are you doing? 你在做什麼?

2. Who's that girl? 那位女孩是誰?

3. I'm too tired to study.
   我太累了,無法讀書。

4. The bus is running late.
   公車要遲到了。

5. I'm taking piano lessons next year.
   我明年要上鋼琴課。

【註】 tired〔taɪrd〕 adj. 累的;疲倦的　　too~to V. 太~而無法
　　　run late 遲到;延誤　　take lessons 上課;聽課

II. 朗讀句子與短文

共有五個句子及一篇短文，請先利用一分
鐘的時間閱讀試卷上的句子與短文，然後
在一分鐘內以正常的速度，清楚正確的朗讀一遍，閱讀時請不要
發出聲音。

One　：　You're staying for lunch, aren't you?
　　　　你會留下來吃午餐，不是嗎？

Two　：　Do you mind if I close the window?
　　　　你介意我關窗戶嗎？

Three：　Sarah bought two kilograms of strawberries at the
　　　　market.　莎拉在市場買了兩公斤的草莓。

Four　：　My older brother graduated from college and is now
　　　　looking for a job.
　　　　我哥哥從大學畢業，現在在找工作。

Five　：　I have an appointment to see the dentist at four
　　　　o'clock.　我和牙醫約四點看診。

【註】stay〔ste〕v. 停留　　mind〔maɪnd〕v. 介意
　　　bought〔bɔt〕v. 買【buy 的過去式】
　　　kilogram〔'kɪlə,græm〕n. 公斤
　　　strawberry〔'strɔ,bɛrɪ〕n. 草莓
　　　graduate〔'grædʒu,et〕v. 畢業
　　　college〔'kɑlɪdʒ〕n. 大學　　***look for***　尋找
　　　appointment〔ə'pɔɪntmənt〕n. 約定；約診

Six　：　Cats are easy pets to care for.　Unlike dogs, cats don't need a lot of exercise.　The best way to keep your cat happy and healthy is to keep it well-fed. Cats like fresh food and prefer to follow a routine. Don't make big changes to their food or feeding schedule.

貓咪是很容易照顧的寵物。不像狗，貓不需要很多運動。要讓你的貓咪高興又健康，最好的方法就是餵飽牠。貓咪喜歡新鮮的食物，而且喜歡遵循慣例。不要對牠們的食物或餵食的計畫做太大的改變。

【註】　pet〔pɛt〕n. 寵物　　***care for*** 照顧
　　　　unlike〔ʌn'laɪk〕prep. 不像
　　　　exercise〔'ɛksəˌsaɪz〕n. 運動
　　　　healthy〔'hɛlθɪ〕adj. 健康的
　　　　well-fed〔'wɛl'fɛd〕adj. 吃得好的；營養充足的
　　　　fresh〔frɛʃ〕adj. 新鮮的
　　　　prefer〔prɪ'fɝ〕v. 偏好；比較喜歡
　　　　follow〔'falo〕v. 遵守；依循
　　　　routine〔ru'tin〕n. 慣例；常規
　　　　make changes to 改變
　　　　feeding〔'fidɪŋ〕adj. 飼養的；供食的
　　　　schedule〔'skɛdʒul〕n. 計畫；行程

Ⅲ. 回答問題

共七題。題目不印在試卷上，由耳機播出，
每題播出兩次，兩次之間大約有一至二秒的
間隔。聽完兩次後，請馬上回答。每題回答時間爲 15 秒，回答
時不一定要用完整的句子，請在作答時間內儘量的表達。

1. **Q**：Do you enjoy swimming? Why or why not?
   你喜歡游泳嗎？爲何喜歡，爲何不喜歡？

   A：Yeah, swimming is great. I love the water.
   是的，游泳很棒。我喜歡水。

   【註】 enjoy〔ɪnˋdʒɔɪ〕v. 喜愛
   yeah〔jæ〕interj. 是（= yes）

2. **Q**：What do you usually do on Saturday nights?
   你週六晚上通常做什麼？

   A：Not much. I usually hang out with my friends and
   walk around.
   沒做什麼。我通常和朋友一起出去玩，到處走。

   【註】 usually〔ˋjuʒʊəlɪ〕adv. 通常
   not much 不多；很少
   hang out 出去玩；消磨時間

3. **Q**：When was the last time you rode the MRT?
   Where did you go?
   你上次搭捷運是什麼時候？你去哪？

A : I rode the MRT today. I came here.

我今天搭了捷運。我來這裡。

【註】 *last time* 上一次

rode〔rod〕*v.* 搭乘【ride 的過去式】

MRT 大眾捷運（= *Mass Rapid Transit*）

4. **Q** : Have you ever had a job? If so, what did you do?

你曾經有過工作嗎？如果有，你做什麼？

A : I have never had a job.

我從來沒有工作過。

【註】 job〔dʒɑb〕*n.* 工作

if so 要是如此（= *if that is the case*）

5. **Q** : How does your family celebrate the New Year?
Do you travel?

你們家慶祝新年嗎？你們去旅遊嗎？

A : We celebrate like most families. We visit my
grandparents in Taichung.

我們跟大部分家庭一樣慶祝。我們去台中探訪祖父母。

【註】 celebrate〔'sɛlə,bret〕*v.* 慶祝

travel〔'trævl̩〕*v.* 旅行　　visit〔'vɪzɪt〕*v.* 探訪

grandparents〔'græn,pɛrənts〕*n. pl.* 祖父母

6. **Q** : How much money do you have in your pocket right
now?

你現在口袋裡有多少錢？

A : I have $500NT in my pocket right now.

我現在口袋裡有新台幣 500 元。

【註】pocket〔'pakɪt〕*n.* 口袋　　***right now*** 現在
　　　NT$ 新台幣（= *New Taiwan dollar*）

7. **Q** : You're sitting next to a new student from a foreign
　　　country. Ask him some questions.

你現在正坐在一個來自外國的學生旁邊。問他一些問題。

A : Where are you from? Why are you in Taiwan?
　　　Do you like it here? How long have you been here?
　　　How long will you stay in Taiwan?

你來自哪裡？你為何在台灣？你喜歡這裡嗎？你在這裡
多久了？你會待在台灣多久？

【註】***next to*** 在…旁邊　　foreign〔'fɔrɪn〕*adj.* 外國的
　　　country〔'kʌntrɪ〕*n.* 國家　　***like it here*** 喜歡這裡

*請將下列自我介紹的句子再唸一遍：

My seat number is （複試座位號碼後 5 碼）, and my test
number is （初試准考證號碼後 5 碼）.

初級英語檢定複試測驗② 詳解

寫作能力測驗詳解

第一部份：單句寫作

第1~5題：句子改寫

1. Amy played basketball with her friends.

   When _____?

   > 重點結構：過去式的 wh- 問句
   >
   > 解　　答：<u>When did Amy play basketball with her friends?</u>
   >
   > 句型分析：When + did + 主詞 + 原形動詞？
   >
   > 説　　明：這一題應將過去式直述句改為 wh- 問句，除了要加
   > 助動詞 did，還要記得助動詞後的動詞須用原形動
   > 詞，因此 played 要改成 play。

2. Watching American movies on TV helps me learn English.

   It _____.

   > 重點結構：以 It 為虛主詞引出的句子
   >
   > 解　　答：<u>It helps me learn English to watch American</u>
   > <u>movies on TV.</u>
   >
   > 句型分析：It + 動詞 + to V.
   >
   > 説　　明：虛主詞 it 代替不定詞片語，不定詞片語則擺在句
   > 尾，故 watching American movies on TV 改
   > 為 to watch American movies on TV。

3. Bob　　：Did you remember to feed the dog?
　　Sarah　：Yes, I did.
　　Sarah remembered _____.

　　　重點結構：「remember + to V」的用法
　　　解　答：Sarah remembered to feed the dog.
　　　句型分析：主詞 + remember + to V
　　　説　明：「記得要去做某事」用 remember + to V，此題
　　　　　　　須在 remember 之後加動名詞，表示已經做了某
　　　　　　　件事情，並且記得。
　　　* feed〔fid〕v. 餵

4. How does Joseph go to school?
　　I don't know _____.

　　　重點結構：間接問句做名詞子句
　　　解　答：I don't know how Joseph goes to school.
　　　句型分析：I don't know + how + 主詞 + 動詞
　　　説　明：在 wh- 問句前加 I don't know，形成間接問句，
　　　　　　　必須把動詞 go 放在最後面，又因主詞 Joseph 為
　　　　　　　第三人稱單數，go 須加 es，並把問號改成句點。

5. Jason cleaned the classroom.（用被動式）
　　The classroom _____.

　　　重點結構：被動語態字序
　　　解　答：The classroom was cleaned by Jason.
　　　句型分析：主詞 + be 動詞 + 過去分詞 + by + 受詞

說　明：一般被動語態的結構是「主詞 + be 動詞 + 過去
　　　　分詞」，按照句意為過去式，又 The classroom
　　　　為第三人稱單數，所以 be 動詞用 was。

第 6～10 題：句子合併

6. Megan asked Carrie something.
Mark was late for school today. (用 why)

_____.

　重點結構：名詞子句當受詞用
　解　答：<u>Megan asked Carrie why Mark was late for
　　　　　school today.</u>
　句型分析：主詞 + 動詞 + why + 主詞 + 動詞
　說　明：Megan 要問 Carrie 一件事情，這件事就是關於
　　　　　Mark 今天上學遲到的事情，兩句之間用 why 來合
　　　　　併。若是直接問句，則 Megan 問 Carrie, "Why
　　　　　was Mark late for school today?"，現在要改為
　　　　　間接問句，即「疑問詞 + 主詞 + 動詞」的形式，在
　　　　　Megan asked Carrie 後面接 why Mark was late
　　　　　for school today，並把問號改為句點。

7. We visited Boston.
We visited New York. (用 both…and～)

_____.

　重點結構：both A and B 的用法
　解　答：<u>We visited both Boston and New York.</u>

句型分析：主詞 + 動詞 + both + 名詞 + and + 名詞

說　明：句意是「我們不但遊覽了波士頓，還有紐約」，
用「both…and～」合併兩個受詞，表「不僅…
而且～」。

* visit〔'vɪzɪt〕v. 參觀

8. The TV program is exciting.
Danny watches the TV program again. (用 enough)

_____.

重點結構：enough 的用法
解　答：<u>The TV program is exciting enough for Danny</u>
<u>to watch again.</u>

句型分析：主詞 + be 動詞 + 形容詞 + enough + for + 受詞 +
to V.

說　明：這題的意思是說「這電視節目夠刺激，所以丹尼再
看一遍」，副詞 enough「足夠地」須置於形容詞
之後，「足以～」則以不定詞表示。

* program〔'progræm〕n. 節目
exciting〔ɪk'saɪtɪŋ〕adj. 刺激的

9. Here is a magazine.
I enjoy the magazine very much. (用 which)

_____.

重點結構：由 which 引導的形容詞子句
解　答：<u>Here is a magazine which I enjoy very much.</u>

句型分析：Here is a magazine + which + 主詞 + 動詞

　說　明：句意是「這是一本我很愛看的雜誌」，在合併兩句時，用 which 代替先行詞 a magazine，引導形容詞子句，在子句中做受詞。

* magazine〔͵mægəˊzin〕n. 雜誌

10. The farmer sold fruit.
　　The farmer made a lot of money.（用 by）

　　_____.

重點結構：「by + V-ing」的用法

　解　答：<u>The farmer made a lot of money by selling fruit.</u>

句型分析：The farmer made a lot of money + by + 動名詞

　說　明：這題的意思是說「這位農夫靠賣水果賺了很多錢」，用「by + V-ing」，表「藉由～（方法）」。

* fruit〔frut〕n. 水果　　***make money*** 賺錢

第 11～15 題：重組

11. Children _____.
　　presents / mothers / on / their / buy / Mother's Day

重點結構：「buy + *sb.* + *sth.*」的用法

　解　答：<u>Children buy their mothers presents on Mother's Day.</u>

句型分析：buy + 間接受詞（人）+ 直接受詞（物）

說　明：「買東西給某人」有兩種寫法：「buy + *sb.* + *sth.*」
或「buy + *sth.* + for + *sb.*」，由於所列出的單字中
沒有 for，這題重組只能用第一種寫法，又「on +
特定日子」，置於句尾，形成此句。

* present〔'prɛznt〕*n.* 禮物

12. Here _____.

the / comes / bus

　　重點結構：Here 置於句首的用法

　　解　答：<u>Here comes the bus.</u>

　　句型分析：Here + 動詞 + 主詞（一般名詞）

　　說　明：這題的意思是說「公車來了」，原本是 The bus
comes here.，Here 置於句首為加強語氣的用法，
若主詞為一般名詞時，須與動詞倒裝。

13. Tina _____.

studied / two / for / English / has / years

　　重點結構：現在完成式字序

　　解　答：<u>Tina has studied English for two years.</u>

　　句型分析：主詞 + have/has + 過去分詞

　　說　明：一般現在完成式的結構是「主詞 + have/has +
過去分詞」，而「for + 一段時間」，表「持續
（多久）」，此時間片語通常置於句尾。

14. Peter asked Jean _____.
she / a / boyfriend / had / whether

> 重點結構：whether 的用法
>
> 解　答：Peter asked Jean whether she had a boyfriend.
>
> 句型分析：Peter asked Jean + whether + 主詞 + 動詞 + 受詞
>
> 説　明：whether 引導名詞子句，做動詞 asked 的受詞，表 「是否」。
>
> * boyfriend〔'bɔɪ,frɛnd〕n. 男朋友

15. Jimmy _____.
such / everyone / a / boy / him / handsome / loves / is / that

> 重點結構：「such…that」的用法
>
> 解　答：Jimmy is such a handsome boy that everyone loves him.
>
> 句型分析：主詞 + be 動詞 + such + 名詞 + that + 主詞 + 動詞
>
> 説　明：這題的意思是說「吉米長得很帥，所以每個人都喜 歡他」，合併兩句時，用「such…that～」，表 「如此…以致於～」。
>
> * handsome〔'hænsəm〕adj. 英俊的

第二部份：段落寫作

題目：今天是除夕夜，你 / 妳許下新年新希望。請根據以下的圖片
　　　寫一篇約 50 字的短文。

　　　I always make some resolutions *on Chinese New Year's Eve*. I want to be healthier, kinder, and happier *next year*. *So* I promise to exercise more and to stay away from fast food. I *also* promise to be kind to everyone that I meet. I will try to help other people as much as I can. *Finally*, I promise to smile more *next year*. With a smile on my face, I can be happy and make other people happy, too. I hope I can keep my resolutions this year.

　　　我總是在除夕夜許一些願望。明年我想要更健康、更善良，並更快樂。所以我答應要多加運動，並遠離速食。我也答應要體貼對待我遇到的人。我會試著盡可能幫助他人。最後，明年我答應要有更多微笑。臉上帶著微笑，我能高興，並也使他人高興。我希望我今年可以達成心願。

resolution〔͵rɛzə'luʃən〕 *n.* 決心要做的事
Chinese New Year's Eve 中國農曆新年除夕夜
healthy〔'hɛlθɪ〕 *adj.* 健康的　　kind〔kaɪnd〕 *adj.* 親切的
promise〔'prɑmɪs〕 *v.* 答應；保證
exercise〔'ɛksə͵saɪz〕 *v.* 運動
stay away from 遠離 (= *keep away from*)　　*fast food* 速食
as much as one *can* 儘量 (= *as much as possible*)
smile〔smaɪl〕 *v. n.* 微笑
keep a resolution 做到決心要做的事

口說能力測驗詳解

*請在 15 秒內完成並唸出下列自我介紹的句子：

My seat number is （複試座位號碼後 5 碼），and my test
number is （初試准考證號碼後 5 碼）.

I. 複誦

共五題。題目不印在試卷上，由耳機播出，
每題播出兩次，兩次之間大約有一至二秒
的間隔。聽完兩次後，請馬上複誦一次。

1. Stop it! 住手！

2. Who was at the door? 誰在門口？

3. I think this is our stop.
   我覺得我們到站了。

4. He has many interesting stories.
   他有很多有趣的故事。

5. Let's meet at noon in front of the train station.
   我們中午在火車站前見面吧。

【註】 ***stop it*** 停止；住手；夠了
　　　door〔dor〕*n.* 門口　　　stop〔stɑp〕*n.* 停車站
　　　interesting〔ˋɪntərɪstɪŋ〕*adj.* 有趣的
　　　story〔ˋstorɪ〕*n.* 故事　　　meet〔mit〕*v.* 見面
　　　in front of 在…的前面　　　***train station*** 火車站

II. 朗讀句子與短文

共有五個句子及一篇短文，請先利用一分
鐘的時間閱讀試卷上的句子與短文，然後

在一分鐘內以正常的速度，清楚正確的朗讀一遍，閱讀時請不要
發出聲音。

One : Jeff is a good athlete, isn't he?

傑夫是個很棒的運動員，不是嗎？

Two : Our neighbors have a small wooden birdhouse in
their backyard.

我們鄰居的後院有一個小的木製鳥籠。

Three : Last year Susie traveled to the home of a famous
musician who died one hundred years ago.

去年蘇西去探訪一位逝世一百年且有名的音樂家的房子。

Four : He lives in a house on a hill with a nice view of the
town below.

他住在一個山丘上的房子，可以一覽山下城鎮的美景。

Five : We're short of a few players today. Care to join us?

我們今天缺少幾個選手。想要加入我們嗎？

【註】 athlete〔ˋæθlɪt〕n. 運動員　　neighbor〔ˋnebɚ〕n. 鄰居
wooden〔ˋwʊdṇ〕adj. 木製的
birdhouse〔ˋbɝd͵haʊs〕n. 鳥屋；鳥籠
backyard〔ˋbæk͵jɑrd〕n. 後庭；後院

famous〔'feməs 〕adj. 有名的
musician〔 mju'zıʃən 〕n. 音樂家
hill〔 hıl 〕n. 小山;山丘　　view〔 vju 〕n. 景觀
below〔 bə'lo 〕adv. 在下方　**be short of** 缺少
player〔'pleə 〕n. 選手　　care〔 kɛr 〕v. 想要

Six ： A bicycle is powered by the rider.　You use your
feet and legs to create motion.　It is good exercise,
and since it doesn't create any pollution, it's good
for the environment, too.　Most people learn to ride
one of these when they are still young, but they are
very popular with people of all ages.

腳踏車由騎士提供動力。你用你的腳和腿來創造動能。這
是很好的運動,而且因為這不會造成任何污染,這對環境
也很好。大多人當他們還年輕時學習騎腳踏車,但是它們
受到各個年齡層人們的歡迎。

【註】 bicycle〔'baı,sıkl̩ 〕n. 腳踏車
power〔'pauə 〕v. 供以⋯動力
rider〔'raıdə 〕n. 騎手;騎士　　use〔 juz 〕v. 使用
create〔 krı'et 〕v. 創造　　motion〔'moʃən 〕n. 動;運動
exercise〔'ɛksə,saız 〕n. 運動　　since〔 sıns 〕conj. 因為
pollution〔 pə'luʃən 〕n. 污染
environment〔 ın'vaırənmənt 〕n. 環境
popular〔'pɑpjələ 〕adj. 受歡迎的 < with >
of all ages 各個年齡層的

III. 回答問題

共七題。題目不印在試卷上，由耳機播出，
每題播出兩次，兩次之間大約有一至二秒的
間隔。聽完兩次後，請馬上回答。每題回答時間為 15 秒，回答
時不一定要用完整的句子，請在作答時間內儘量的表達。

1. **Q**：What kind of movies do you like?
   你喜歡什麼類型的電影？

   A：I like comedies, mostly. 我喜歡的大多是喜劇。

   【註】kind〔kaɪnd〕*n.* 種類　　comedy〔ˋkɑmədɪ〕*n.* 喜劇
   　　　mostly〔ˋmostlɪ〕*adv.* 大概；多半

2. **Q**：How much time do you spend on the Internet every
   day? 你每天花多少時間上網？

   A：I probably spend about two hours a day on the Internet.
   我可能一天花兩個小時上網。

   【註】Internet〔ˋɪntəˌnɛt〕*n.* 網際網路
   　　　probably〔ˋprɑbəblɪ〕*adv.* 可能

3. **Q**：What's your favorite subject at school?
   你在學校最愛的科目是什麼？

   A：English composition is definitely my favorite subject
   in school.
   英文作文確定是我在學校最愛的科目。

   【註】favorite〔ˋfevərɪt〕*adj.* 最喜愛的
   　　　subject〔ˋsʌbdʒɪkt〕*n.* 科目

composition〔͵kɑmpə'zɪʃən〕*n.* 作文
definitely〔'dɛfənɪtlɪ〕*adv.* 確實；一定

4. **Q**：Who is your best friend? What is he or she like?

   誰是你最好的朋友？他或她是怎樣的人？

   A：My best friend is named Drew. He's a very funny and witty character.

   我最好的朋友名叫德魯。他是個好笑又機智的人。

   【註】name〔nem〕*v.* 命名　　funny〔'fʌnɪ〕*adj.* 逗人發笑的
   witty〔'wɪtɪ〕*adj.* 機智的
   character〔'kærɪktə〕*n.* 人格；人物

5. **Q**：What did you have for breakfast this morning?

   你今天早上早餐吃什麼？

   A：I didn't eat breakfast this morning because I was running late. 我今天早上沒吃早餐，因為我快遲到了。

   【註】breakfast〔'brɛkfəst〕*n.* 早餐
   be running late 快遲到了

6. **Q**：What would you do if you saw someone stealing from a convenience store?

   如果你看到有人在便利商店偷竊，你會怎麼做？

   A：I would tell the store's manager about what I had seen so they could check the CCTV.

   我會告訴店經理關於我所看到的，如此他們就會去查看閉路電視。

【註】 steal〔stil〕v. 偷 <from>
convenience〔kən'vinjəns〕n. 便利
convenience store 便利商店
manager〔'mænɪdʒɚ〕n. 經理
check〔tʃɛk〕v. 檢查;查看
CCTV 閉路電視 (= Closed-Circuit Television)

7. **Q**: Your friend Tom just failed a big exam. Give him
some words of encouragement.

你的朋友湯姆剛有一個大考不及格。對他說一些鼓勵的話。

A: Hey, Tom. Don't take it so hard. You tried your best.
There will be other exams. Come on, cheer up.

嘿,湯姆。看開點。你盡力了。還會有其他的考試。快點,
振作起來。

【註】 just〔dʒʌst〕adv. 剛剛　　fail〔fel〕v. 考不及格
exam〔ɪg'zæm〕n. 考試　　words〔wɝds〕n. pl. 話語
encouragement〔ɪn'kɝɪdʒmənt〕n. 鼓勵
take sth. **hard** 對某事感到難過
try one's **best** 盡某人所能
come on (表示鼓勵) 來吧;快點
cheer up 鼓起精神;振作起來

* 請將下列自我介紹的句子再唸一遍:

My seat number is ＿（複試座位號碼後 5 碼）＿, and my test
number is ＿（初試准考證號碼後 5 碼）＿.

初級英語檢定複試測驗③詳解

寫作能力測驗詳解

第一部份：單句寫作

第 1~5 題：句子改寫

1. Getting a lot of lucky money is a happy thing.
   It's _____.

   重點結構：以 It 為虛主詞引出的句子

   解　答：It's a happy thing to get a lot of lucky money.

   句型分析：It's + 名詞 + to V.

   說　明：It 代替不定詞片語做主詞，不定詞片語則擺在句尾，故 getting a lot of lucky money 改為 to get a lot of lucky money。

   * lucky〔'lʌkɪ〕 *adj.* 幸運的　***lucky money*** 壓歲錢

2. I made my dog sit down.
   My dog _____ by me.

   重點結構：動詞 make 被動語態的用法

   解　答：My dog was made to sit down by me.

   句型分析：主詞 + be 動詞 + made + to V.

   說　明：「make + 受詞 + 原形 V.」表「叫～做…」，若改為被動語態，原形動詞須改為不定詞。

3. I will never forget the good time we spent together.

Never _____.

  重點結構：never 置於句首的用法

   解 答：<u>Never will I forget the good time we spent together.</u>

  句型分析：Never + 助動詞 + 主詞 + 原形動詞

   說 明：never 為否定副詞，置於句首加強語氣時，主詞與動詞須倒裝。

4. It rains a lot in winter in Taipei.

We _____.

  重點結構：rain 的用法

   解 答：<u>We have a lot of rain in winter in Taipei.</u>

  句型分析：We + have + rain + 時間副詞 + 地方副詞

   說 明：表「下雨」的說法有三種：

       It *rains*.（rain 是動詞）

       We have *rain*.（rain 是不可數名詞）

       There is *rain*.（rain 是不可數名詞）

      a lot 是副詞片語，表「許多」，修飾動詞，若要修飾名詞，須改為 a lot of，表「許多的」。

5. I spent two hours cleaning my bedroom.

It _____.

  重點結構：take 的用法

   解 答：<u>It took me two hours to clean my bedroom.</u>

句型分析：It takes + *sb.* + to V.

說　明：「花費時間」的用法：

$\left\{\begin{array}{l} 人 + spend + 一段時間 + V\text{-}ing \\ 事物或 It + take + 人 + 一段時間 + to\ V. \end{array}\right.$

spent 是過去式動詞，故 take 要改成過去式動詞 took，cleaning 要改成不定詞 to clean。

* bedroom〔ˈbɛd,rum〕*n.* 臥室

第 6～10 題：句子合併

6. Study hard.

You will get good grades.（用 and）

_____.

重點結構：祈使句表達條件句的用法

解　答：<u>Study hard, and you will get good grades.</u>

句型分析：祈使句, and + 主詞 + 動詞

說　明：此句型表「如果…，就～」。本句可改為：

If you study hard, you will get good grades.

7. I want to know the girl.

That girl has short hair.（用 with 合併）

_____.

重點結構：with 的用法

解　答：<u>I want to know the girl with short hair.</u>

句型分析：I want to know the girl + with + 名詞

　　説　明：介系詞 with 在此表「有」，相當於 having。

　　　　　　with short hair 用來修飾 the girl。

8. The coffee is very hot.

　 I can't drink it.（用 so…that 合併）

_____.

　重點結構：so…that～ 的用法

　　解　答：The coffee is so hot that I can't drink it.

　句型分析：主詞 + be 動詞 + so + 形容詞 + that 子句

　　説　明：這題的意思是說「咖啡太燙，所以我沒辦法喝」。

　　　　　　用 so…that～ 合併兩句，表「如此…以致於～」。

9. I didn't see you yesterday.

　 I didn't see you the day before yesterday.（用 either 合併）

　 I didn't _____, and I didn't _____.

　重點結構：either 的用法

　　解　答：I didn't see you yesterday, and I didn't (see

　　　　　　you) the day before yesterday(,) either.

　句型分析：主詞 + 動詞，and + 主詞 + 動詞 + (,) either.

　　説　明：否定句的「也」，用 either，擺在句尾，之前的

　　　　　　逗號可寫，也可不寫。

　* *the day before yesterday* 前天

10. A man wants to see you.

    The man is called Dr. Wang. (用 who 合併)

    A man who _____.

    重點結構：由 who 引導的形容詞子句

    解　答：<u>A man who is called Dr. Wang wants to see you.</u>

    句型分析：A man ＋ who ＋ 動詞 ＋ 名詞 ＋ 動詞

    說　明：這題的意思是說「有位王醫生想要見你」，在合併時，用 who 代替先行詞 A man，引導形容詞子句。

    * call 〔 kɔl 〕 v. 稱為

第 11～15 題：重組

11. What _____?

    she / usually / does / do / Sundays / on

    重點結構：wh- 問句的用法

    解　答：<u>What does she usually do on Sundays?</u>

    句型分析：What ＋ 助動詞 ＋ 主詞 ＋ 動詞？

    說　明：What 引導的問句中，主詞為第三人稱單數，故助動詞用 does，而不是 do；頻率副詞 usually 置於助動詞 does 之後，一般動詞 do 之前。

    * *on Sundays* 每個星期天 (= *every Sunday*)

12. Would _____?

kind / to give / a / enough / you / me / be / hand

重點結構：enough 的用法

解　答：<u>Would you be kind enough to give me a hand?</u>

句型分析：be 動詞 + 形容詞 + enough + to V.

説　明：這題的意思是說「你能不能好心點，幫我一個忙？」
副詞 enough 須置於形容詞之後，後面再接不定詞
片語，表「夠…，足以～」。

* kind〔kaɪnd〕*adj.* 好心的
give sb. a hand 幫助某人（= *help sb.*）

13. I _____.

to / frightened / too / open / my / am / eyes

重點結構：「too + 形容詞 + to V.」的用法

解　答：<u>I am too frightened to open my eyes.</u>

句型分析：主詞 + be 動詞 + too + 形容詞 + to V.

説　明：這題的意思是說「我太害怕了，不敢張開眼睛」，
用 too…to V. 合併，表「太…以致於不～」。

* frightened〔ˈfraɪtn̩d〕*adj.*（人）害怕的

14. Our teacher _____.

how / teaches / to / us / sing / songs / English

重點結構：teach 的用法

解　答：<u>Our teacher teaches us how to sing English</u>
　　　　<u>songs.</u>

句型分析：主詞 + teach + 受詞 + 疑問詞 + to V.

説　明：teach 的用法為：

$$\begin{cases} \text{teach} + sb. + sth. \\ \text{teach} + sth. + \text{to} + sb. \end{cases}$$

所列出的單字中，to 是不定詞的 to，不是介系詞的
to，故用第一種方式重組。「疑問詞 + to V.」，
構成「名詞片語」，做動詞 teaches 的受詞。

15. It ＿＿＿＿＿＿＿＿＿＿＿＿＿＿＿＿＿＿＿＿＿＿.
must / frightening / to / a ghost / be / see

重點結構：以 It 為虛主詞引出的句子

解　答：<u>It must be frightening to see a ghost.</u>

句型分析：It + 助動詞 + be 動詞 + 形容詞 + 不定詞

説　明：虛主詞 it 代替不定詞片語，不定詞片語 to see a
ghost 則放在句尾，整句的意思是「看見鬼一定很
可怕」。

* must〔mʌst〕*aux.* 一定
frightening〔'fraɪtn̩ɪŋ〕*adj.* 可怕的
ghost〔gost〕*n.* 鬼

第二部份：段落寫作

題目：昨天妳/你和姐姐及她的男朋友去看恐怖片（horror movie）。請根據以下的圖片寫一篇約 50 字的短文。

Yesterday was a holiday. I went to the movies with my sister and her boyfriend. I wanted to see the new cartoon movie and my sister wanted to see a love story, **but** her boyfriend wanted to see a horror movie. He bought the tickets, so we went to see the scary movie. I was scared to death during the movie. I covered my eyes and screamed. **Finally**, it was over.

When I went to bed, I couldn't forget the movie. I kept thinking about the ghost and stayed awake all night. **Next time** I go to the movies, I will not choose a horror movie.

昨天是假日。我和我姊姊以及她的男朋友去看電影。我想要看新的卡通，而我姊姊想要看愛情故事，但是她的男朋友想要看恐怖片。他買了票，所以我們去看恐怖片。我在看電影的時候嚇得要死。我遮住眼睛並尖叫。最後，電影結束了。

當我上床睡覺，我無法忘記那部電影。我一直想著鬼，而整晚沒睡。下次我去看電影的時候，我不會選擇恐怖片。

go to the movies 去看電影　　cartoon〔kɑr'tun〕*n.* 卡通
horror movie 恐怖片（= *scary movie*）
scary〔'skɛrɪ〕*adj.* 可怕的　　scare〔skɛr〕*v.* 驚嚇
be scared to death 嚇得要死；非常害怕
cover〔'kʌvɚ〕*v.* 覆蓋　　scream〔skrim〕*v.* 尖叫
finally〔'faɪnḷɪ〕*adv.* 最後；終於　　keep〔kip〕*v.* 持續
stay〔ste〕*v.* 保持　　awake〔ə'wek〕*adj.* 清醒的
choose〔tʃuz〕*v.* 選擇

口説能力測驗詳解

*請在15秒內完成並唸出下列自我介紹的句子：

My seat number is （複試座位號碼後5碼）, and my test number is （初試准考證號碼後5碼）.

I. 複誦

共五題。題目不印在試卷上，由耳機播出，
每題播出兩次，兩次之間大約有一至二秒的
間隔。聽完兩次後，請馬上複誦一次。

1. It's hot today. 今天很熱。

2. I'm thirsty. 我口渴。

3. My little brother drives me crazy.
   我弟弟讓我發瘋。

4. You've been very kind.
   你一直都很善良。

5. Thanks for all your help.
   謝謝你所有的幫助。

【註】 thirsty〔ˈθɝstɪ〕 *adj.* 口渴的　　drive〔draɪv〕 *v.* 使
crazy〔ˈkrezɪ〕 *adj.* 發瘋的　　kind〔kaɪnd〕 *adj.* 善良的
thanks for 謝謝～　　help〔hɛlp〕 *n.* 幫助

II. 朗讀句子與短文

共有五個句子及一篇短文，請先利用一分
鐘的時間閱讀試卷上的句子與短文，然後
在一分鐘內以正常的速度，清楚正確的朗讀一遍，閱讀時請不要
發出聲音。

One : Sarah saw a movie with her friends last night.

莎拉昨晚和她的朋友們一起看電影。

Two : They went to the police station to ask for help.

他們去警察局求助。

Three : Dave used to work in a bookstore, but now he works in a bank.

戴夫以前在書店工作，但現在他在銀行工作。

Four : Jack spent $1,000NT on snacks at the night market.

傑克花了台幣一千元買夜市小吃。

Five : My brother Tom is studying overseas. He will come home for Chinese New Year.

我哥哥湯姆正在國外讀書。他農曆新年會回家。

【註】 *see a movie* 看電影　　*police station* 警察局
ask for 要求；請求　　*used to V.* 以前～
bookstore〔'buk‚stor〕*n.* 書店　　bank〔bæŋk〕*n.* 銀行
snack〔snæk〕*n.* 點心；小吃　　*night market* 夜市
overseas〔'ovɚ'siz〕*adv.* 在海外；在國外
Chinese New Year 中國農曆新年

Six　：Jimbo's is having a special sale. When you buy three muffins, we will give you a fourth one free. Choose from a wide range of flavors including chocolate, blueberry, and our specialty, peanut butter. Also, we are offering 10 percent off on all cakes, pies, and cookies.

金波正在特賣。當你買三個瑪芬蛋糕，我們會免費贈送第四個。從各種口味中挑選，包含巧克力、藍莓，以及我們的招牌商品，花生醬口味。而且，我們目前蛋糕、派，和餅乾打九折。

【註】 special〔ˈspɛʃəl〕*adj.* 特別的　　sale〔sel〕*n.* 銷售；特價
muffin〔ˈmʌfɪn〕*n.* 瑪芬蛋糕　　free〔fri〕*adv.* 免費地
choose from 從⋯選擇
a wide range of 廣泛的；各種的
flavor〔ˈflevɚ〕*n.* 味道；風味
including〔ɪnˈkludɪŋ〕*prep.* 包含
chocolate〔ˈtʃɔklɪt〕*n.* 巧克力
blueberry〔ˈbluˌbɛrɪ〕*n.* 藍莓
specialty〔ˈspɛʃəltɪ〕*n.* 特產　　peanut〔ˈpiˌnʌt〕*n.* 花生
peanut butter 花生醬　　also〔ˈɔlso〕*adv.* 此外
offer〔ˈɔfɚ〕*v.* 提供　　percent〔pɚˈsɛnt〕*n.* 百分比
cake〔kek〕*n.* 蛋糕　　pie〔paɪ〕*n.* 派
cookie〔ˈkʊkɪ〕*n.* 餅乾

III. 回答問題

共七題。題目不印在試卷上，由耳機播出，
每題播出兩次，兩次之間大約有一至二秒的

間隔。聽完兩次後，請馬上回答。每題回答時間為 15 秒，回答
時不一定要用完整的句子，請在作答時間內儘量的表達。

1. **Q**：Have you ever been sick? How did you feel?

   你曾經生病過嗎？你感覺如何？

   A：I get sick all the time. I usually feel lousy.

   我總是在生病。我通常覺得很不舒服。

   【註】sick〔sɪk〕*adj.* 生病的

   　　　get〔gɛt〕*v.* 變得　　***all the time*** 一直；總是

   　　　usually〔ˈjuʒʊəlɪ〕*adv.* 通常

   　　　lousy〔ˈlaʊzɪ〕*adj.* 很糟的；很不舒服的

2. **Q**：What do you usually buy at the night market?
   What's your favorite snack?

   你通常在夜市買什麼？你最喜愛的宵夜是什麼？

   A：I usually buy these spicy pork buns, which are my
   favorite snack, at the night market.

   我通常買這些辣味割包，這是我在夜市最愛的宵夜。

   【註】***night market*** 夜市

   　　　favorite〔ˈfevərɪt〕*adj.* 最喜愛的

   　　　snack〔snæk〕*n.* 點心；宵夜

   　　　spicy〔ˈspaɪsɪ〕*adj.* 辣的　　pork〔pɔrk〕*n.* 豬肉

   　　　bun〔bʌn〕*n.* 小圓麵包　　***pork bun*** 割包

3. **Q** : How much sleep do you get? Do you think it's enough?

你睡多少？你覺得這夠嗎？

A : I get seven to eight hours of sleep a night. I think that's enough.

我一晚睡七到八小時。我覺得那足夠了。

【註】 sleep〔slip〕 n. 睡眠　　enough〔ɪˋnʌf〕adj. 足夠的

4. **Q** : Have you ever traveled? Where did you go?

你曾經去旅遊嗎？你去過哪裡？

A : I've traveled many places including the U.S. and Europe. 我去過很多地方旅遊，包含美國和歐洲。

【註】 travel〔ˋtrævl〕v. 旅遊
　　　including〔ɪnˋkludɪŋ〕prep. 包含
　　　the U.S. 美國 (= *the United States*)
　　　Europe〔ˋjʊrəp〕n. 歐洲

5. **Q** : What do you think about owning pets? Do you have one? 你覺得養寵物如何？你有養嗎？

A : I guess owning a pet is OK. I don't have one.

我想養寵物是沒問題的。我沒有養。

【註】 own〔on〕v. 擁有　　pet〔pɛt〕n. 寵物

6. **Q** : When did you last play a sport? What did you play and who did you play with?

你上次運動是什麼時候？你做什麼運動，和誰一起運動？

A： I played basketball with my friends last weekend.

我上個週末和我朋友們一起打籃球。

【註】last〔læst〕*adv.* 上次；最近　　***play a sport*** 運動

weekend〔'wik‚ɛnd〕*n.* 週末

7. **Q：** Your friend Dave wasn't in school last week. Ask him why.

你的朋友戴夫上個禮拜沒有來上學。問他原因。

A： Hey, Dave, why weren't you in school today? Are you OK? Is there any problem?

嘿，戴夫，為什麼你今天沒有來上學。你還好嗎？有任何問題嗎？

【註】*in shool* 上學

＊請將下列自我介紹的句子再唸一遍：

My seat number is （複試座位號碼後 5 碼）, and my test number is （初試准考證號碼後 5 碼）.

初級英語檢定複試測驗 ④ 詳解

寫作能力測驗詳解

第一部份：單句寫作

第 1~5 題：句子改寫

1. What color does Lily like the best?

   Please tell me _____.

   > 重點結構：間接問句做名詞子句
   >
   > 解　　答：<u>Please tell me what color Lily likes the best.</u>
   >
   > 句型分析：Please tell me + what color + 主詞 + 動詞
   >
   > 說　　明：在 wh- 問句前加 Please tell me，須改為間接問句，把動詞 like 放在主詞 Lily 的後面，又因主詞為第三人稱單數，like 須加 s，並把問號改成句點。
   >
   > * color〔'kʌlɚ〕*n.* 顏色

2. Mr. and Mrs. Robinson usually go to the gym after work.

   Where _____?

   > 重點結構：現在式的 wh- 問句
   >
   > 解　　答：<u>Where do Mr. and Mrs. Robinson usually go after work?</u>
   >
   > 句型分析：Where + do + 主詞 + 動詞

説　明：這一題應將現在式直述句改為 wh- 問句，除了加助動詞 do，還要記得助動詞後面要用原形動詞 go。

* gym〔dʒɪm〕n. 健身房　　**after work** 下班後

3. Mother：Did you do the dishes?

Peter　：Oh, I forgot.

Peter forgot _____.

重點結構：「forget + to V.」的用法

解　答：Peter forgot to do the dishes.

句型分析：主詞 + forget + to V.

説　明：「忘記去做某件事」用 forget + to V. 來表達，此題須在 forget 之後加不定詞。

* **do the dishes** 洗碗

4. To bring a dead man back to life is impossible.

It's _____.

重點結構：以 It 為虛主詞引出的句子

解　答：It's impossible to bring a dead man back to life.

句型分析：It's + 形容詞 + to V.

説　明：虛主詞 It 代替不定詞片語，不定詞片語 to bring a dead man back to life 則擺在句尾。

* **bring sb. back to life** 使某人復活

dead〔dɛd〕adj. 死亡的

impossible〔ɪm'pɑsəbl〕adj. 不可能的

5. Put on your sweater. (…it…)

  _____.

　　重點結構：put on 的用法

　　　解　答：<u>Put it on.</u>

　　句型分析：put + 代名詞 + on

　　　説　明：put on「穿上」為可分片語，故「穿上毛衣。」有
　　　　　　　兩種寫法，即 Put on your sweater. 或 Put your
　　　　　　　sweater on. 若用代名詞 it 代替 your sweater，則
　　　　　　　只能放在 put 跟 on 的中間。

第 6～10 題：句子合併

6. I go to the library.
   I return the books. (用 to)

  _____.

　　重點結構：不定詞的用法

　　　解　答：<u>I go to the library to return the books.</u>

　　句型分析：I go to the library + to V.

　　　説　明：這題的意思是說「我去圖書館還書」。用不定詞
　　　　　　　來合併兩句，不定詞在此表目的。

　　* return〔rɪ'tɝn〕v. 歸還

7. I will meet Sarah tonight.
   I'll give her the CD. (用 when)
   I'll give Sarah _____.

重點結構：未來式的 wh- 子句

解　答：<u>I'll give Sarah the CD when I meet her tonight.</u>

句型分析：I'll give Sarah the CD + when + 主詞 + 動詞

說　明：在表時間的副詞子句中，要用現在式代替未來式，所以雖然「我今晚會與 Sarah 會面」是未來的時間，但不能寫成 when I *will meet* Sarah tonight，須用 when I *meet* Sarah tonight。

* meet〔mit〕*v.* 會面

8. We can go on a picnic.

The weather is nice.（用 as long as）

We can _____.

重點結構：as long as 的用法

解　答：<u>We can go on a picnic as long as the weather is nice.</u>

句型分析：主詞 + 動詞 + as long as + 主詞 + 動詞

說　明：這題的句意是「我們可以去野餐，只要天氣好的話」，as long as「只要」爲連接詞片語，故後面要接完整的子句，即主詞加動詞的形式。

* weather〔'wɛðɚ〕*n.* 天氣

9. Mary is very young.

Mary cannot go to school.（用 too…to）

_____.

重點結構：「too + 形容詞 + to V.」的用法

解　　答：<u>Mary is too young to go to school.</u>

句型分析：主詞 + be 動詞 + too + 形容詞 + to V.

說　　明：這題的意思是說「瑪麗年紀太小，還不能上學」，用 too…to V. 合併，表「太…以致於不～」。

* young〔jvŋ〕*adj.* 年輕的

10. I have a good friend.

My good friend sings well. (用 who)

_____.

重點結構：由 who 引導的形容詞子句

解　　答：<u>I have a good friend who sings well.</u>

句型分析：I have a good friend + who + 動詞

說　　明：這題的意思是說「我有一位很會唱歌的朋友」，在合併時，用 who 代替先行詞 a good friend，引導形容詞子句。

第 11～15 題：重組

11. Mike _____?

his mother / to take out / helped / the garbage

重點結構：「help + *sb.* + to V.」的用法

解　　答：<u>Mike helped his mother to take out the garbage.</u>

句型分析：help + 受詞 + 不定詞

　　　　　說　明：這題的意思是「我幫媽媽倒垃圾」，help 的用法
　　　　　　　　　 是接受詞後，須接不定詞或原形動詞。

　　* **take out** 拿出去
　　　 garbage〔'gɑrbɪdʒ〕*n.* 垃圾

12. Did _____?
　　 have / cake / dessert / for / you

　　　重點結構：一般過去式問句的用法
　　　　解　答：Did you have cake for dessert?
　　　句型分析：Did + 主詞 + 原形動詞？
　　　　說　明：這題是說「你有吃蛋糕，作為餐後甜點嗎？」，
　　　　　　　　 have 在此表示「吃」的意思。

　　* cake〔kek〕*n.* 蛋糕
　　　 dessert〔dɪ'zɜt〕*n.* 餐後甜點

13. Martha _____.
　　 late / never / for / is / school

　　　重點結構：never 的用法
　　　　解　答：Martha is never late for school.
　　　句型分析：主詞 + be 動詞 + never
　　　　說　明：never 為頻率副詞，須置於 be 動詞的後面。

　　* late〔let〕*adj.* 遲到的

14. Wendy _____.

so / that / studies / gets / hard / she / grades / good

> 重點結構：「so + 形容詞 + that 子句」的用法
>
> 解　答：Wendy studies so hard that she gets good grades.
>
> 句型分析：主詞 + 動詞 + so + 副詞 + that + 主詞 + 動詞
>
> 説　明：這題的意思是說「溫蒂非常用功唸書，所以她得到好成績」，合併兩句時，用「so…that~」，表「如此…以致於~」。
>
> * hard〔hɑrd〕adv. 努力地
> grade〔gred〕n. 成績

15. How _____?

coffee / would / like / you / your

> 重點結構：wh- 問句的用法
>
> 解　答：How would you like your coffee?
>
> 句型分析：How + 助動詞 + 主詞 + 動詞
>
> 説　明：整句的意思是「你想要怎麼樣的咖啡？」，是問人要不要加糖或奶精的說法。
>
> * coffee〔ˈkɔfɪ〕n. 咖啡

第二部份：段落寫作

題目： 昨天是弟弟/哥哥的生日。請根據以下的圖片寫一篇約 50 字
的短文。

Yesterday was my brother's birthday. *In the morning*
my mother and I went to a bakery. We bought a delicious
cake. *In the afternoon* we went shopping for a present. We
found a cool sweater. It was on sale, so it was not too
expensive. *Last night* we all sang Happy Birthday to my
brother. We had a wonderful birthday party.

昨天是我弟弟的生日。早上，我媽媽和我去麵包店。我們買了
一個好吃的蛋糕。下午我們去買了一個禮物。我們發現了一件很酷
的毛衣。它正在特價，所以不會太貴。昨晚，我們所有人唱生日快
樂歌給我弟弟。我們有個很棒的生日派對。

bakery〔ˋbekərɪ〕n. 麵包店   *shop for* ~ 去買~
present〔ˋprɛznt〕n. 禮物   sweater〔ˋswɛtɚ〕n. 毛衣
on sale 特價中   wonderful〔ˋwʌndəfəl〕adj. 很棒的

口說能力測驗詳解

*請在15秒內完成並唸出下列自我介紹的句子：

My seat number is （複試座位號碼後5碼）, and my test number is （初試准考證號碼後5碼）.

I. 複誦

共五題。題目不印在試卷上，由耳機播出，每題播出兩次，兩次之間大約有一至二秒的間隔。聽完兩次後，請馬上複誦一次。

1. Have a seat. 請坐。

2. It's great to see you again. 很高興再次見到你。

3. Why is that girl crying?
   爲何女孩在哭泣？

4. I really like this song!
   我眞的很喜歡這首歌！

5. It might rain, so you'd better carry an umbrella with you.
   可能會下雨，所以你最好帶把雨傘。

【註】 seat〔sit〕n. 座位　　song〔sɔŋ〕n. 歌曲
　　　 rain〔ren〕v. 下雨　　***had better V***. 最好～
　　　 carry〔ˋkærɪ〕v. 攜帶　　umbrella〔ʌmˋbrɛlə〕n. 雨傘

II. 朗讀句子與短文

共有五個句子及一篇短文，請先利用一分
鐘的時間閱讀試卷上的句子與短文，然後
在一分鐘內以正常的速度，清楚正確的朗讀一遍，閱讀時請不要
發出聲音。

One : The toy shop is on the corner. You can't miss it.
玩具店在轉角。你不會錯過的。

Two : Can I borrow 20 dollars until we find an ATM?
在我們找到自動櫃員機前，我可以借個 20 元嗎？

Three : The tourists are taking photographs from the bridge.
旅客正從橋上拍照。

Four : Among all the animals in this zoo, the monkey is
one of the cutest.
在動物園裡面所有的動物中，猴子是最可愛的之一。

Five : Many people are in the temple praying for health
and happiness in the new year.
很多人在廟裡面祈求在新的一年中健康快樂。

【註】 toy〔tɔɪ〕n. 玩具　　shop〔ʃɑp〕n. 商店
corner〔'kɔrnɚ〕n. 轉角　　miss〔mɪs〕v. 錯過；沒看到
borrow〔'bɔro〕v. 借入
ATM 自動櫃員機（ = *automated-teller machine*）
tourist〔'tʊrɪst〕n. 觀光客；旅客　　***take a picture*** 照相
bridge〔brɪdʒ〕n. 橋　　zoo〔zu〕n. 動物園

monkey〔'mʌŋkɪ〕*n.* 猴子　　temple〔'tɛmpḷ〕*n.* 廟
pray〔pre〕*v.* 祈禱　　health〔hɛlθ〕*n.* 健康
happiness〔'hæpɪnɪs〕*n.* 幸福；快樂

Six　　：In Taipei, there are dozens of public libraries where people can borrow books for free. Not that long ago, libraries did not exist in the city. People had to borrow books from private libraries. These libraries rented books to people for short periods of time.

在台北，有很多市立圖書館，人們可以在這裡免費借書。
不久前，這個城市還沒有圖書館。人們必須去私立圖書館借書。這些圖書館短期出租書給人們。

【註】dozen〔'dʌzṇ〕*n.* 一打；十二個　　***dozens of*** 很多
public〔'pʌblɪk〕*adj.* 公共的；公立的
library〔'laɪ‚brɛrɪ〕*n.* 圖書館　　***for free*** 免費
exist〔ɪg'zɪst〕*v.* 存在
private〔'praɪvɪt〕*adj.* 私人的；私立的
rent〔rɛnt〕*v.* 出租　　period〔'pɪrɪəd〕*n.* 期間

III. 回答問題

共七題。題目不印在試卷上，由耳機播出，
每題播出兩次，兩次之間大約有一至二秒的
間隔。聽完兩次後，請馬上回答。每題回答時間為 15 秒，回答
時不一定要用完整的句子，請在作答時間內儘量的表達。

1. **Q**: When was the last time you went to a party?
   Who was the host?
   你上一次去派對是什麼時候？誰是主辦人？

   A: I went to a girl's birthday party last year. It was
   hosted by this other girl, Mary.
   我去年去一個女孩的派對。是由另一個女孩主辦的，瑪麗。

   【註】*last time* 上一次
   　　　host〔host〕*n.* 主人；主辦人　*v.* 主辦

2. **Q**: Do you have a special talent? What is it?
   你有特別的才能嗎？是什麼？

   A: I do have a special talent. I can run very fast.
   我真的有一個特別的才能。我能跑很快。

   【註】special〔'spɛʃəl〕*adj.* 特別的　　talent〔'tælənt〕*n.* 才能
   　　　do + V. 的確~；真的~　　run〔rʌn〕*v.* 跑

3. **Q**: What kind of animals do you like?
   你喜歡什麼種類的動物？

   A: I love cats, but I like all animals in general except for
   bugs and snakes.

我喜歡貓，但是一般來說我喜歡所有的動物，除了蟲和蛇。

【註】 kind〔kaɪnd〕*n.* 種類　　*in general* 一般來說；大體上
except for 除了　　bug〔bʌg〕*n.* 蟲
snake〔snek〕*n.* 蛇

4. Q：Would you be interested in learning to play a musical
　　instrument? Which one?
　　你對學習彈奏樂器有興趣嗎？哪一個？

A：I would love to learn how to play piano.
　　我想要學彈鋼琴。

【註】 *be interested in* 對…感興趣　　play〔ple〕*v.* 彈奏
musical〔'mjuzɪkl̩〕*adj.* 音樂的
instrument〔'ɪnstrəmənt〕*n.* 工具；樂器
would love to V. 想要～　　piano〔pɪ'æno〕*n.* 鋼琴

5. Q：Describe your favorite meal. Include a main dish,
　　side dish, dessert, and beverage. 描述你最喜歡的
　　餐點。包含主菜、配菜、飯後甜點，和飲料。

A：My favorite meal is a double cheeseburger, large fries,
　　apple pie, and a chocolate shake. 我最喜歡的餐點是雙
　　層起司漢堡、大薯、蘋果派，和巧克力奶昔。

【註】 describe〔dɪ'skraɪb〕*v.* 描述
meal〔mil〕*n.* 一餐　　include〔ɪn'klud〕*v.* 包含
main〔men〕*adj.* 主要的　　dish〔dɪʃ〕*n.* 食物；菜餚
side dish 配菜；小菜　　dessert〔dɪ'zɝt〕*n.* 飯後甜點
beverage〔'bɛvərɪdʒ〕*n.* 飲料
double cheeseburger 雙層起司漢堡
fries〔fraɪz〕*n. pl.* 薯條　　shake〔ʃek〕*n.* 奶昔

6. **Q** : What would you do if you saw an old man struggling to cross a busy intersection?

   如果你看到一位老先生努力要穿過一個熱鬧的十字路口，你會怎麼做？

   A : I would stop and help him across the street.

   我會停下來並幫他穿過街道。

   【註】 struggle〔ˈstrʌgḷ〕v. 掙扎；奮力
   cross〔krɔs〕v. 跨過　　busy〔ˈbɪzɪ〕adj. 熱鬧的
   intersection〔ˌɪntəˈsɛkʃən〕n. 十字路口
   across〔əˈkrɔs〕prep. 跨過；橫跨

7. **Q** : Your friend Mike is upset. Say something to cheer him up.

   你的朋友麥可很難過。說些什麼來鼓舞他。

   A : Hey, Mike. Don't be down. I'm here for you. Tell me all your troubles.

   嘿，麥可。別沮喪。我在這幫你。告訴我所有你的煩惱。

   【註】 upset〔ʌpˈsɛt〕adj. 難過的　　***cheep up*** 鼓舞；振奮
   down〔daʊn〕adj. 沮喪的；難過的
   trouble〔ˈtrʌbḷ〕n. 煩惱

*請將下列自我介紹的句子再唸一遍：

My seat number is （複試座位號碼後 5 碼）, and my test number is （初試准考證號碼後 5 碼）.

初級英語檢定複試測驗 ⑤ 詳解

寫作能力測驗詳解

第一部份：單句寫作

第 1～5 題：句子改寫

1. When is the next movie?

   Tell us when _____.

   重點結構：間接問句做名詞子句

   解　答：<u>Tell us when the next movie is.</u>

   句型分析：Tell us + when + 主詞 + 動詞

   説　明：在 wh- 問句前加 Tell us，形成間接問句，必須把
   　　　　　be 動詞 is 放在最後面，並把問號改成句點。

2. My backpack is different from yours. (用 the same as)

   _____.

   重點結構：「the same as」的用法

   解　答：<u>My backpack is not the same as yours.</u>

   句型分析：主詞 + be 動詞 + the same as + 所有格代名詞

   説　明：以 not the same as「和～不一樣」取代 different
   　　　　　from。

   * backpack〔ˈbækˌpæk〕 *n.* 背包
     different〔ˈdɪfrənt〕 *adj.* 不同的
     be different from 和～不同
     same〔sem〕 *adj.* 相同的　　***be the same as*** 和～相同

3. Jerry ： Did you bring the comic book?

   Carrie ： Oh, I forgot.

   Carrie forgot ＿＿＿＿＿＿＿＿＿＿＿＿＿ comic book.

   > 重點結構：「forget + to V.」的用法
   >
   > 解　答：Carrie forgot to bring the comic book.
   >
   > 句型分析：主詞 + forget + to V.
   >
   > 説　明：「忘記去做某件事」用 forget + to V. 來表示，此題須在 forgot（forget 的過去式）後面接不定詞。

   * **comic book** 漫畫書

4. To keep a pet is not easy.

   It ＿＿＿＿＿＿＿＿＿＿＿＿＿＿＿＿＿＿＿.

   > 重點結構：以 It 為虛主詞引導的句子
   >
   > 解　答：It is not easy to keep a pet.
   >
   > 句型分析：It is + 形容詞 + to V.
   >
   > 説　明：虛主詞 It 代替不定詞片語，真正的主詞是不定詞片語 to keep a pet，則置於句尾。

   * pet〔pɛt〕*n.* 寵物　　***keep a pet*** 養寵物

5. Mandy went to the gift shop.

   Why ＿＿＿＿＿＿＿＿＿＿＿＿＿＿＿ the gift shop?

   > 重點結構：過去式的 wh- 問句
   >
   > 解　答：Why did Mandy go to the gift shop?
   >
   > 句型分析：Why + did + 主詞 + 原形動詞？

說　明：這一題應將過去式直述句改爲 wh- 問句，除了要
　　　　加助動詞 did，還要記得助動詞後面的動詞，須用
　　　　原形動詞，因此 went 要改成 go。

* *gift shop* 禮品店

第 6～10 題：句子合併

6. Patricia told Joyce something.

John went home late.

Patricia told Joyce why ＿＿＿＿＿＿＿＿＿＿＿＿＿＿＿＿＿.

　　重點結構：名詞子句當受詞用

　　　解　答：<u>Patricia told Joyce why John went home late.</u>

　　句型分析：Patricia told Joyce + why + 主詞 + 動詞

　　　說　明：Patricia 要告訴 Joyce 一件事，就是關於 John 晚
　　　　　　　回家這件事，兩句之間用疑問詞 why 來合併，如果
　　　　　　　是直接問句的話，我們會說："Why did John go
　　　　　　　home late?"，但這裡前面有 Patricia told Joyce，
　　　　　　　因此後面必須接名詞子句，做爲 Patricia told
　　　　　　　Joyce 的受詞，即「疑問詞 + 主詞 + 動詞」的形
　　　　　　　式，在 Patricia told Joyce 後面接 why John went
　　　　　　　home late。

7. I have a dog.

My dog is sleeping right now. (用 that)

I have a dog that ＿＿＿＿＿＿＿＿＿＿＿＿＿＿＿＿＿.

　　重點結構：由 that 引導的形容詞子句

解　答：I have a dog that is sleeping right now.

句型分析：I have a dog + that + 動詞

說　明：句意是「我有一隻狗，現在牠正在睡覺」，在合併
兩句時，用 that 代替先行詞 a dog，引導形容詞子
句，在子句中做主詞。

* **_right now_** 現在（ = _now_ ）

8. We moved the piano.
   My neighbors helped us.
   My neighbors helped us _____.

重點結構：「help + _sb._ + (to) V.」的用法

解　答：My neighbors helped us (to) move the piano.

句型分析：help + 受詞 + 原形動詞或不定詞

說　明：句意是「我的鄰居幫我們搬鋼琴」，用動詞 help
造句，help 之後所接的不定詞的 to 可省略。

* neighbor〔'nebɚ〕_n._ 鄰居
move〔muv〕_v._ 搬動

9. I went to the Museum of Fine Arts.
   I took the bus there. (用 by)
   I went _____ by _____.

重點結構：「by + 交通工具」的用法

解　答：I went to the Museum of Fine Arts by bus.

句型分析：主詞 + 動詞 + by + 名詞

説　明：這題的意思是說「我搭公車去美術館」，用「by +
交通工具」，表「搭乘～（交通工具）」，注意交
通工具不能加定冠詞 the。

* museum〔mju'ziəm〕*n.* 博物館　　*fine arts* 美術

10. Linda is very old.

Linda cannot see well. (用 too…to)

Linda is too old _____.

重點結構：「too + 形容詞 + to V.」的用法

解　答：<u>Linda is too old to see well.</u>

句型分析：主詞 + be 動詞 + too + 形容詞 + to V.

説　明：這題的意思是說「琳達年紀太大，看不清楚」，用
too…to V. 合併這兩句，表「太…以致於不～」。

第 11～15 題：重組

11. Would _____.

like / tea / cup / you / to have / a / of

重點結構：「Would you like + to V.?」的用法

解　答：　<u>Would you like to have a cup of tea?</u>

句型分析：Would you like + 不定詞？

説　明：「Would you like～?」為徵詢某人是否要某物
的用法，比「Do you want～?」更普遍，且更
有禮貌。

12. Nancy _____.

most / questions / can / difficult / the / answer

重點結構：形容詞最高級的用法

解　答：<u>Nancy can answer the most difficult questions.</u>

句型分析：the most + 形容詞

說　明：difficult 為兩個音節以上的形容詞，故前面加
　　　　　most，形成最高級。

* answer〔'ænsɚ〕v. 回答
difficult〔'dıfə,kʌlt〕adj. 困難的
question〔'kwɛstʃən〕n. 問題

13. The weather _____.

so / I / stay / that / is / hot / would rather / inside

重點結構：「so + 形容詞 + that 子句」的用法

解　答：<u>The weather is so hot that I would rather stay</u>
　　　　　<u>inside.</u>

句型分析：主詞 + be 動詞 + so + 形容詞 + that + 主詞 + 動詞

說　明：這題的意思是說「天氣太熱了，所以我寧願待在屋
　　　　　內」，合併兩句時，用「so…that~」，表「如此
　　　　　…以致於~」。

* weather〔'wɛðɚ〕n. 天氣
would rather + 原形 V. 寧願
stay〔ste〕v. 停留；保持
inside〔'ın'saıd〕adv. 在室內

14. Paul _____.

has / sick / for / a / been / month

重點結構：現在完成式字序

解　答：<u>Paul has been sick for a month.</u>

句型分析：主詞 + have/has + been + 形容詞 + for + 一段時間

說　明：一般現在完成式的結構是「主詞 + have/has + 過去
分詞」，be 動詞的現在完成式是 have/has been，
而「for + 一段時間」，表「持續（多久）」，此時
間片語置於句尾。

* sick〔sɪk〕*adj.* 生病的

15. Kay _____.

afraid / taking / tests / is / of / English / not

重點結構：「be 動詞 + afraid + of + 動名詞」的用法

解　答：<u>Kay is not afraid of taking English tests.</u>

句型分析：主詞 + be 動詞 + afraid + of + 動名詞

說　明：afraid（害怕的）的用法為：

{ be 動詞 + afraid of + N / V-ing
  be 動詞 + afraid + that + 主詞 + 動詞

從 taking 可知，此題重組是第一種用法。

* afraid〔ə'fred〕*adj.* 害怕的

第二部份：段落寫作

題目：請根據以下的圖片寫一篇約 50 字的短文。

One morning my mother asked me to carry an umbrella to school. She said it would rain. *But* it was a sunny morning. I did not believe her, and I did not want to take an umbrella. I said "No!" loudly and went to school.

That afternoon it rained. The rain was heavy. I got wet because I did not have an umbrella. *That night* I began to cough and sneeze. I had caught a cold. *Next time* I will listen to my mother.

有一天早上，我媽媽要要我上學帶一把傘。她說說會下雨。但是早晨是晴天。我不相信她，並沒有帶雨傘。我大聲說「不」，就去上學了。

那天下午下雨了。雨很大。因為沒有帶雨傘，我淋濕了。那天晚上，我開始咳嗽和打噴嚏。我感冒了。下一次我會聽我母親的話。

carry〔ˈkærɪ〕*v.* 攜帶　　umbrella〔ʌmˈbrɛlə〕*n.* 雨傘
rain〔ren〕*v.* 下雨　　sunny〔ˈsʌnɪ〕*adj.* 陽光普照的
believe〔bɪˈliv〕*v.* 相信　　loudly〔ˈlaʊdlɪ〕*adv.* 大聲地
heavy〔ˈhɛvɪ〕*adj.* 大量的　　wet〔wɛt〕*adj.* 濕的
cough〔kɔf〕*v.* 咳嗽　　sneeze〔sniz〕*v.* 打噴嚏
catch a cold 感冒　　*next time* 下一次　　*listen to* 聽從

口說能力測驗詳解

＊請在 15 秒內完成並唸出下列自我介紹的句子：

My seat number is （複試座位號碼後 5 碼）, and my test number is （初試准考證號碼後 5 碼）.

I. 複誦

共五題。題目不印在試卷上，由耳機播出，每題播出兩次，兩次之間大約有一至二秒的間隔。聽完兩次後，請馬上複誦一次。

1. Have a look at this. 看一下這個。

2. This bicycle is not safe to ride. 這腳踏車騎起來不安全。

3. That's my neighbor, Mr. Chen.
   那位是我的鄰居，陳先生。

4. It takes ten minutes to walk home from school.
   走到學校要花十分鐘。

5. I'd like to travel to Europe.
   我想要去歐洲旅行。

【註】 *have a look at* 看一下　　bicycle〔ˈbaɪˌsɪkḷ〕*n.* 腳踏車
safe〔sef〕*adj.* 安全的　　ride〔raɪd〕*v.* 騎
neighbor〔ˈnebɚ〕*n.* 鄰居　　Mr.〔ˈmɪstɚ〕*n.* …先生
take〔tek〕*v.* 花（時間）　　*would like to V.* 想要~
travel〔ˈtrævḷ〕*v.* 旅行　　Europe〔ˈjurəp〕*n.* 歐洲

II. 朗讀句子與短文

共有五個句子及一篇短文，請先利用一分
鐘的時間閱讀試卷上的句子與短文，然後
在一分鐘內以正常的速度，清楚正確的朗讀一遍，閱讀時請不要
發出聲音。

One : Things were quiet until the Johnson family moved
in next door.
一切都很平靜，直到強生一家人搬到隔壁。

Two : As a result, many people were injured in car
accidents.
因此，很多人在車禍中受傷。

Three : You seem worried. Is something wrong?
你看起來很憂慮。發生什麼事嗎？

Four : What do you think of the concert so far?
到目前為止你覺得這演唱會如何？

Five : Kevin turned on the gas stove and started to boil
some water.
凱文打開瓦斯爐並開始燒水。

【註】 things〔θɪŋz〕*n. pl.* 事態；情況
quiet〔ˈkwaɪət〕*adj.* 安靜的；平靜的
as a result 因此　　injure〔ˈɪndʒɚ〕*v.* 傷害
accident〔ˈæksədənt〕*n.* 意外

think of 認為　　concert〔'kɑnsɝt〕*n.* 演唱會
so far 到目前為止　　*turn on* 打開（電器等）
stove〔stʌv〕*n.* 爐子　　*gas stove* 瓦斯爐
boil〔bɔɪl〕*v.* 煮沸；燒開

Six　：No one can run as fast as Charles. He's the fastest
　　　　guy around. He wins every race he enters. He has
　　　　won more athletic awards than any other kid in
　　　　school.

　　　　沒有人跑得跟查爾斯一樣快。他是這裡跑最快的人。
　　　　他每場參加的比賽都獲勝。他贏的運動獎項比這學校
　　　　的任何其他孩童都多。

【註】 fast〔fæst〕*adv.* 快速地　　guy〔gaɪ〕*n.*（男）人
　　　 around〔ə'raʊnd〕*adv.* 周圍；附近
　　　 race〔res〕*n.* 比賽　　enter〔'ɛntɚ〕*v.* 進入；參加
　　　 won〔wʌn〕*v.* 贏【win 的過去分詞】
　　　 athletic〔æθ'lɛtɪk〕*adj.* 體育的；運動的
　　　 award〔ə'wɔrd〕*n.* 獎　　kid〔kɪd〕*n.* 小孩

III. 回答問題

共七題。題目不印在試卷上，由耳機播出，
每題播出兩次，兩次之間大約有一至二秒的
間隔。聽完兩次後，請馬上回答。每題回答時間爲 15 秒，回答
時不一定要用完整的句子，請在作答時間內儘量的表達。

1. **Q**：Do you have any siblings?
   你有任何兄弟姊妹嗎？

   A：I have two sisters and a brother.
   我有兩個姊姊和一個弟弟。

   【註】sibling〔ˈsɪblɪŋ〕*n.* 兄弟姊妹

2. **Q**：Where do you live? What's the exact address?
   你住哪裡？確切的地址是什麼？

   A：I live in Taipei at No. 15, Lane 223, Fuxing South
   Road, Section 3.
   我住在台北市，復興南路三段，223 巷，15 號。

   【註】exact〔ɪgˈzækt〕*adj.* 準確的
   address〔ˈædrɛs〕*n.* 地址
   No. 號碼（= *number*）   lane〔len〕*n.* 巷子
   section〔ˈsɛkʃən〕*n.* 部分；（路）段

3. **Q**：Do your parents enjoy eating at restaurants or
   cooking at home?
   你的父母喜歡在餐廳吃飯還是在家煮飯？

A： They enjoy both. Sometimes we eat out; sometimes we eat at home.

他們兩個都喜歡。有時候我們在外面吃飯；有時候我們在家吃。

【註】 parents〔'pɛrənts〕*n. pl.* 父母
enjoy〔ɪn'dʒɔɪ〕*v.* 喜歡
restaurant〔'rɛstərənt〕*n.* 餐廳
sometimes〔'sʌm,taɪmz〕*adv.* 有時候

4. **Q**： Have you taken a vacation recently?

你最近有休假嗎？

A： I have not taken a vacation recently.

我最近沒有休假。

【註】 vacation〔ve'keʃən〕*n.* 休假　　***take a vacation*** 休假
recently〔'risṇtlɪ〕*adv.* 最近

5. **Q**： What's the weather like today?

今天天氣如何？

A： It's kind of cool and overcast, with occasional rain.

有點涼意且多雲偶陣雨。

【註】 weather〔'wɛðɚ〕*n.* 天氣　　***kind of*** 有一點
cool〔kul〕*adj.* 涼爽的；微冷的
overcast〔'ovɚ,kæst〕*adj.* 多雲的
occasional〔ə'keʒənḷ〕*adj.* 偶爾的　　rain〔ren〕*n.* 雨

6. **Q**： What are you planning to do this weekend?

你這個週末計畫做什麼？

A： I'm planning to study and maybe go to the bookstore.

我打算要讀書並去書店。

【註】 plan〔plæn〕v. 計畫；打算　　study〔'stʌdɪ〕v. 讀書

weekend〔'wik'ɛnd〕n. 週末

maybe〔'mebɪ〕adv. 可能

bookstore〔'bʊk,stor〕n. 書店

7. **Q**： Your friend Larry has a part-time job. Ask him some questions about the job.

你的朋友賴瑞有一份兼職的工作。問他一些關於這份工作的問題。

A： What do you do? How much do you make? How often do you work? Do you like the job?

你的工作是什麼？你收入多少？你多久去上一次班？你喜歡這份工作嗎？

【註】 part-time〔'part,taɪm〕adj. 兼職的

job〔dʒab〕n. 工作　　***how often*** 多久一次

work〔wɝk〕n. 工作

＊請將下列自我介紹的句子再唸一遍：

My seat number is （複試座位號碼後 5 碼）, and my test number is （初試准考證號碼後 5 碼）.

初級英語檢定複試測驗 ⑥ 詳解

寫作能力測驗詳解

第一部份：單句寫作

第 1~5 題：句子改寫

1. Paula asked me, "Could you lend me your umbrella?"
   Paula asked me if ＿＿＿＿＿＿ lend her my umbrella.

   > 重點結構：直接問句改為間接問句的用法
   >
   > 解　答：<u>Paula asked me if I could lend her my umbrella.</u>
   >
   > 句型分析：Paula asked me + if + 主詞 + 動詞
   >
   > 説　明：Could you lend me your umbrella? 是直接問句，
   > 現在要放在 if「是否」後面，做為 Paula asked
   > me 的受詞，即名詞子句（間接問句）「連接詞 +
   > 主詞 + 動詞」的形式，在 Paula asked me 後面接
   > if I could lend her my umbrella，並把問號改成
   > 句點。
   >
   > * lend〔lɛnd〕v. 借（出）　　umbrella〔ʌm'brɛlə〕n. 雨傘

2. Frank is taller than all the other students in his class.
   Frank ＿＿＿＿＿＿ tallest ＿＿＿＿＿＿ in his class.

   > 重點結構：比較級表達最高級的用法
   >
   > 解　答：<u>Frank is the tallest student in his class.</u>
   >
   > 句型分析：主詞 + be 動詞 + the + 形容詞最高級 + 名詞

　　　　　　說　　明：題目的意思是「法蘭克比他班上的其他學生高」，
　　　　　　　　　　　換句話說，「法蘭克是他班上最高的學生」，可以
　　　　　　　　　　　用最高級表達，在 tallest 之前須加定冠詞 the，並
　　　　　　　　　　　把 students 改爲單數名詞 student。

3. Andy overslept, so he was late for school.

　　Andy ＿＿＿＿＿＿＿＿＿ because ＿＿＿＿＿＿＿＿＿＿＿.

　　重點結構：because 的用法

　　解　　答：<u>Andy was late for school because he overslept.</u>

　　句型分析：主詞＋動詞＋ because ＋主詞＋動詞

　　說　　明：連接詞 so（所以）和 because（因爲）的比較：

　　　　　　　　　　原因＋ so ＋結果
　　　　　　　　　　結果＋ because ＋原因

　　＊ oversleep〔'ovɚ'slip〕v. 睡過頭　　　late〔let〕adj. 遲到的

4. Matt will go to junior high school.

　　When ＿＿＿＿＿＿＿＿＿＿＿＿＿＿＿＿＿＿＿＿＿＿＿＿？

　　重點結構：未來式的 wh- 問句

　　解　　答：<u>When will Matt go to junior high school?</u>

　　句型分析：When ＋ will ＋主詞＋原形動詞？

　　說　　明：這一題應將未來式直述句改爲 wh- 問句，疑問詞
　　　　　　　　後面要加表未來的助動詞 will。

5. Nancy watches cartoons every night.

　　Nancy ＿＿＿＿＿＿＿＿＿＿＿＿＿＿＿＿＿ last night.

重點結構：過去式動詞

　解　答：<u>Nancy watched cartoons last night.</u>

句型分析：主詞 + 動詞 + 時間副詞

　說　明：時間副詞 every night 改爲 last night，動詞要
　　　　　改爲過去式，watches 改成 watched。

* cartoon〔kɑr'tun〕*n.* 卡通

第 6～10 題：句子合併

6. May likes to listen to music.
   May also likes to go climbing.
   May likes to _____.

　重點結構：and 的用法

　　解　答：<u>May likes to listen to music and (to) go</u>
　　　　　　<u>climbing.</u>

　　　或　　<u>May likes to go climbing and (to) listen to</u>
　　　　　　<u>music.</u>

　句型分析：主詞 + 動詞 + 不定詞 + and + 不定詞或原形動詞

　　說　明：and 是對等連接詞，連接兩個不定詞，做動詞
　　　　　　likes 的受詞，而第二個不定詞的 to 可省略。

　* *go climbing* 去爬山

7. How much does it cost?
   I don't know.
   I don't know how _____.

　重點結構：間接問句做名詞子句

解　　答：I don't know how much it costs.

句型分析：I don't know + how + 主詞 + 動詞

說　　明：在 wh- 問句前加 I don't know，形成間接問句，
即「疑問詞 + 主詞 + 動詞」的形式，必須把動詞
cost 放在最後面，因為 it 是第三人稱單數，故
cost 須加 s，並把問號改成句點。

8. Tim has cats.

Eva is Tim's cat.

Eva ＿＿＿＿＿＿＿＿ one of ＿＿＿＿＿＿＿＿＿＿＿＿＿＿＿＿＿.

重點結構：「one of + 所有格 + 複數名詞」的用法

解　　答：Eva is one of Tim's cats.

句型分析：主詞 + be 動詞 + one of + 所有格 + 複數名詞

說　　明：題目的意思是「伊娃是提姆的貓當中的一隻」，
「～當中的一個」用「one of + 複數名詞」來
表示，cat 須用複數形。

9. Fred is 155cm tall.

Robert is 155cm tall, too.

Fred ＿＿＿＿＿＿＿＿＿＿＿＿＿＿＿＿＿＿＿＿＿ as Robert.

重點結構：「as…as～」的用法

解　　答：Fred is as tall as Robert.

句型分析：主詞 + be 動詞 + as + 形容詞 + as + 受詞

說　明：這題是說佛瑞德身高一百五十五公分，羅伯特身高
　　　　也是一百五十五公分，所以兩個人長得一樣高，用
　　　　「as…as～」來連接兩句話，表「和～一樣…」。

　* cm　公分（ *centimeter* 的略稱）

10. Judy goes jogging.
　　Then she has breakfast.
　　Judy _____ before _____.

　重點結構：before 的用法
　　解　答：Judy goes jogging before she has breakfast.
　　　或　　Judy goes jogging before (having) breakfast.
　句型分析：主詞＋動詞＋before＋主詞＋動詞
　　　或　　主詞＋動詞＋before＋（動）名詞
　　說　明：then「然後」表示茱蒂先慢跑，再吃早餐，現在
　　　　　　用 before「在～之前」來表示事情的先後順序。
　　　　　　而 before 有兩種詞性，若作為連接詞，引導副詞
　　　　　　子句時，須接完整的主詞與動詞，即 before she
　　　　　　has breakfast；若作為介系詞，後面須接名詞或
　　　　　　動名詞，即 before breakfast 或 before having
　　　　　　breakfast。

　* *go jogging*　去慢跑

第 11～15 題：重組

11. Kelly _____.
　　been learning / has / for / karate / seven years

重點結構：現在完成進行式字序

解　答：<u>Kelly has been learning karate for seven years.</u>

句型分析：主詞 + have/has been + 現在分詞 + for + 一段時間

說　明：現在完成進行式的結構是「主詞 + have/has been + 現在分詞」，而「for + 一段時間」，表「持續（多久）」，此時間片語置於句尾。

* karate〔kəˈrɑtɪ〕n. 空手道

12. He _____.

to make / with / my brother / wants / friends

重點結構：「make friends with sb.」的用法

解　答：<u>He wants to make friends with my brother.</u>

句型分析：主詞 + 動詞 + 不定詞片語

說　明：make friends with sb. 表「與某人交朋友」。

13. Iris bought _____.

at the bookstore / this pencil box / the park / next to

重點結構：表地點的介系詞的用法

解　答：<u>Iris bought this pencil box at the bookstore next to the park.</u>

句型分析：主詞 + 動詞 + 受詞 + 地方副詞

說　明：next to the park 修飾 bookstore。

* **pencil box** 鉛筆盒　　bookstore〔ˈbʊkˌstor〕n. 書店
  next to 在…旁邊

14. How many _____?

in the basket / are / eggs / there

重點結構：「How many + 複數名詞 + are there?」的用法

解　答：How many eggs are there in the basket?

句型分析：How many + 複數名詞 + are there + 地方副詞

說　明：「How many + 複數名詞？」表「～有多少？」，
而「there + be 動詞」表「有」，在問句中要倒
裝，故形成 are there，地方副詞 in the basket
則置於句尾。

* egg〔εg〕n. 蛋　　basket〔'bæskɪt〕n. 籃子

15. The _____.

and / sweet / tastes / sour / soup

重點結構：「taste + 形容詞」的用法

解　答：The soup tastes sour and sweet.

　或　　　The soup tastes sweet and sour.

句型分析：主詞 + 動詞 + 形容詞

說　明：動詞 taste「嚐起來」後面須接形容詞做補語，
用對等連接詞 and 連接兩個形容詞。

* soup〔sup〕n. 湯　　taste〔test〕v. 嚐起來
sweet〔swit〕adj. 甜的　　sour〔saʊr〕adj. 酸的

第二部份：段落寫作

題目： 爸爸買了一輛新腳踏車給我，並且教我如何騎腳踏車。經過
不斷的嚐試，我終於學會了。請根據以下的圖片寫一篇約 50
字的短文。

My father gave me a new bike. I was very happy. *But*
I didn't know how to ride it. My father tried very hard to
teach me. I tried again and again, *but* I could not do it. I
even fell and hurt my knee. I hated the new bike.

My father asked me to try one more time. *To my
surprise*, I could ride the bike. I was very happy, and my
father was happy, too.

我爸爸給我一台腳踏車。我很高興。但是我不知道要如何騎。
我爸爸很努力要教我。我一次又一次嘗試，但是我做不到。我甚至
跌倒並傷了膝蓋。我討厭這台新的腳踏車。

我父親要我在嘗試一次。讓我驚訝的，我能夠騎腳踏車了。我
很高興，而我的父親也很高興。

bike〔baɪk〕*n.* 腳踏車　　hard〔hɑrd〕*adv.* 努力地
ride〔raɪd〕*v.* 騎　　*again and again*　一再地
fall〔fɔl〕*v.* 跌落【三態變化為：fall-fell-fallen】
hurt〔hɝt〕*v.* 使受傷【三態同形】　　knee〔ni〕*n.* 膝蓋
hate〔het〕*v.* 討厭　　*ask sb. + to V.* 要求某人做～
to one's surprise 令某人驚訝的是

口說能力測驗詳解

＊請在15秒內完成並唸出下列自我介紹的句子：

My seat number is （複試座位號碼後 5 碼）, and my test
number is （初試准考證號碼後 5 碼）.

I. 複誦

共五題。題目不印在試卷上，由耳機播出，
每題播出兩次，兩次之間大約有一至二秒
的間隔。聽完兩次後，請馬上複誦一次。

1. Sorry, I'm late. 很抱歉，我遲到了。

2. This cake is delicious. 蛋糕很好吃。

3. I found a spelling error on page six.
   我在第六頁發現一個拼字錯誤。

4. Let's go for a walk.
   我們去散步吧。

5. Mr. Smith is on the phone.
   史密斯先生在講電話。

【註】late〔let〕adj. 遲到的　　cake〔kek〕n. 蛋糕
　　　delicious〔dɪ'lɪʃəs〕adj. 美味的
　　　spelling〔'spɛlɪŋ〕adj. 拼字的　　error〔'ɛrə〕n. 錯誤
　　　page〔pedʒ〕n. 頁　　*let's* + *V.* 一起去～吧
　　　go for a walk 去散步　　*on the phone* 講電話

II. 朗讀句子與短文

共有五個句子及一篇短文,請先利用一分
鐘的時間閱讀試卷上的句子與短文,然後
在一分鐘內以正常的速度,清楚正確的朗讀一遍,閱讀時請不要
發出聲音。

One : We should leave the house around seven-thirty in order to beat the traffic.

我們應該在七點三十分離開家以避免塞車。

Two : It's been a fairly cool and dry summer so far, hasn't it?

到目前爲止這個夏天都很涼爽乾燥,不是嗎?

Three : The shopping mall isn't too far from here.

購物中心離這裡不遠。

Four : I have two tickets for tonight's concert.

我有兩張今晚演唱會的票。

Five : If you get hungry there's leftover pizza in the refrigerator you can warm up in the microwave.

如果你餓了,冰箱裡面有剩下的披薩,你可以用微波爐加熱。

【註】 *in order to V.* 爲了~   beat〔bit〕*v.* 打贏;勝過
beat the traffic 避免塞車   fairly〔'fɛrlɪ〕*adv.* 非常
cool〔kul〕*adj.* 涼爽的   *so far* 到目前爲止

shopping mall 購物中心　　ticket〔'tɪkɪt〕*n.* 票
concert〔'kɑnsɝt〕*n.* 演唱會
hungry〔'hʌŋgrɪ〕*adj.* 飢餓的
leftover〔'lɛft‚ovɚ〕*adj.* 剩餘的
microwave〔'maɪkrə‚wev〕*n.* 微波爐（= *microwave oven*）

Six ：The test is about to begin. If you have any problem
　　with the volume of the recording, please raise your
　　hand. You will have 45 minutes to complete the
　　test. Please write your name and seat number at the
　　top of the test. Good luck!

　　考試要開始了。如果你有任何關於錄音音量的問題，請
　　舉手。你將會有四十五分鐘來完成考試。請在考卷上寫
　　下你的名字和座位號碼。祝你好運！

【註】*be about to V.* 即將~；正要~
　　volume〔'vɑljəm〕*n.* 音量
　　recording〔rɪ'kɔrdɪŋ〕*n.* 錄音　　raise〔rez〕*v.* 舉起
　　minute〔'mɪnɪt〕*n.* 分鐘　　complete〔kəm'plit〕*v.* 完成
　　seat〔sit〕*n.* 座位　　*good luck* 祝你好運

Ⅲ. 回答問題

共七題。題目不印在試卷上，由耳機播出，每題播出兩次，兩次之間大約有一至二秒的間隔。聽完兩次後，請馬上回答。每題回答時間為 15 秒，回答時不一定要用完整的句子，請在作答時間內儘量的表達。

1. **Q**：Do you have anything in your pockets?

　　你口袋有什麼東西嗎？

　　A：I have an Easy Card and $3,000 NT in my pocket.

　　我口袋裡有一張悠遊卡和台幣三千元。

　　【註】pocket〔ˋpɑkɪt〕 *n.* 口袋　　***Easy Card*** 悠遊卡

2. **Q**：What do you usually carry in your backpack?

　　你背包通常帶什麼？

　　A：All kinds of stuff. It depends where I'm going, but usually books and school supplies.

　　各種東西。這要看我要去哪，但是通常是書和學校文具用品。

　　【註】usually〔ˋjuʒʊəlɪ〕 *adv.* 通常；一般
　　　　 carry〔ˋkærɪ〕 *v.* 攜帶　　 backpack〔ˋbæk͵pæk〕 *n.* 背包
　　　　 kind〔kaɪnd〕 *n.* 種類　　 stuff〔stʌf〕 *n.* 東西
　　　　 depend〔dɪˋpɛnd〕 *v.* 依靠；取決於
　　　　 supplies〔səˋplaɪz〕 *n. pl.* 供應品

3. **Q**：When was the last time you ate in a restaurant?
　　　　 What did you have?

　　你上一次吃餐廳是什麼時候？你吃了什麼？

A : I ate at a beef noodle shop last night.　I had the beef noodles.

我昨晚在一家牛肉麵店吃飯。我吃了牛肉麵。

【註】 ***last time*** 上一次　　restaurant〔'rɛstərənt〕*n.* 餐廳
have〔hæv〕*v.* 吃；喝　　beef〔bif〕*n.* 牛肉
noodles〔'nudḷz〕*n. pl.* 麵條　　shop〔ʃɑp〕*n.* 商店

4. **Q** : Have you ever lost any money?　How much did you lose?

你曾經弄丟錢嗎？你弄丟多少錢？

A : I once lost $1,000 NT that my grandfather gave me.

我曾經弄丟台幣一千元，那是我祖父給我的。

【註】 lost〔lɔst〕*v.* 弄丟【lose 的過去式】
lose〔luz〕*v.* 弄丟　　once〔wʌns〕*adv.* 曾經
grandfather〔'grænd,faðə〕*n.* 祖父

5. **Q** : Are you able to keep a balance between your school and social life?

你能夠在學校和社交生活達到平衡嗎？

A : Not really.　It's mostly school, with very little time for social activities.

不完全是。大多是學校的事，很少有社交活動的時間。

【註】 ***be able to V.*** 能夠～　　balance〔'bæləns〕*n.* 平衡
keep a balance 保持平衡
social〔'soʃəl〕*adj.* 社會的；社交的
not really 不完全是
mostly〔'mostlɪ〕*adv.* 大多；主要地
activity〔æk'tɪvətɪ〕*n.* 活動

6. **Q**: How would you feel if someone very close to you was very sick and likely to die in the near future?

   如果一位跟你很親近的人生重病，並在不久的未來很可能過世，你會感到如何？

   A: I'd feel really sad about that.

   我會真的因此感到很難過。

   【註】close〔klos〕*adj.* 親近的　　sick〔sɪk〕*adj.* 生病的
   likely〔'laɪklɪ〕*adj.* 可能的　　die〔daɪ〕*v.* 死
   in the near future 在不久的未來
   sad〔sæd〕*adj.* 難過的

7. **Q**: Your friend Monica has a new hairstyle. Ask her about it.

   你的朋友莫妮卡換了一個新髮型。問問她關於此事。

   A: Did you get a new haircut? Where did you get it? Why did you choose that style?

   妳換了新髮型嗎？妳去哪裡剪的？妳為何選擇那個風格？

   【註】hairstyle〔'hɛr,staɪl〕*n.* 髮型
   haircut〔'hɛr,kʌt〕*n.* 剪髮；髮型
   style〔staɪl〕*n.* 風格

＊請將下列自我介紹的句子再唸一遍：

My seat number is （複試座位號碼後 5 碼）, and my test number is （初試准考證號碼後 5 碼）.

初級英語檢定複試測驗 ⑦ 詳解

寫作能力測驗詳解

第一部份：單句寫作

第 1~5 題：句子改寫

1. Two boys are playing badminton at the playground.

   Who _____?

   重點結構：wh- 問句的用法

   解　答：<u>Who is playing badminton at the playground?</u>

   句型分析：Who + be 動詞 + 現在分詞？

   説　明：Who 做主詞時，須視爲單數，故 be 動詞用 is。

   * badminton〔'bædmɪntən〕n. 羽毛球
   playground〔'ple‚graʊnd〕n.（學校的）操場

2. Eating too much is bad for your health.

   It is _____.

   重點結構：以 It 爲虛主詞引導的句子

   解　答：<u>It is bad for your health to eat too much.</u>

   句型分析：It is + 形容詞 + 不定詞

   説　明：虛主詞 It 代替不定詞片語，不定詞片語則置於句
   　　　　尾，故 eating too much 改爲 to eat too much。

   * health〔hɛlθ〕n. 健康

3. I eat and sleep a lot.

   _____ last weekend.

   重點結構：過去式動詞

   　解　答：<u>I ate and slept a lot last weekend.</u>

   句型分析：主詞 + 動詞

   　說　明：由時間副詞 last weekend 可知，動詞須用過去
   　　　　　式，eat 和 sleep 是不規則動詞，其過去式是 ate
   　　　　　和 slept。

   ＊ weekend〔'wik‚ɛnd〕n. 週末

4. My parents bought some comic books for me.

   My parents _____ comic books.

   重點結構：buy 的用法

   　解　答：<u>My parents bought me some comic books.</u>

   句型分析：buy + 間接受詞（人）+ 直接受詞（物）

   　說　明：「買東西給某人」有兩種寫法：
   　　　　　「buy + *sth.* + for + *sb.*」或「buy + *sb.* + *sth.*」。
   　　　　　這題要改成第二種用法，先寫人（me），再寫物
   　　　　　（comic books）。

   ＊ *comic book* 漫畫書

5. "I like your new shoes," I said to Mary.

   I said to Mary that _____.

重點結構：直接引用改為間接引用的用法

解　答：<u>I said to Mary that I liked her new shoes.</u>

句型分析：I said to Mary + that + 主詞 + 動詞

說　明：" "裡面的話是直接引用，若去掉" "，則是間接
引用的用法，即 that 引導的名詞子句，做為動詞
said 的受詞，子句中的動詞要和主要動詞 said 的
時態相同，所以 like 須改成 liked，而所有格 your
是指「瑪麗的」，故在間接引用時，改成 her。

* shoes〔ʃuz〕*n. pl.* 鞋子

第 6～10 題：句子合併

6. Polly can't speak Japanese.

Rita can't speak Japanese.

Neither _____.

重點結構：「neither…nor～」的用法

解　答：<u>Neither Polly nor Rita can speak Japanese.</u>

句型分析：Neither + A + nor + B + 助動詞 + 動詞

說　明：這題是說波莉不會說日文，莉塔也不會說日文，所
以兩個人都不會說日文，用「neither…nor～」來
連接兩個主詞，表「兩者皆不」。

* speak〔spik〕*v.* 說
Japanese〔͵dʒæpə'niz〕*n.* 日語

7. Kevin is very young.

Kevin cannot go to school.

Kevin is too _____.

　　重點結構：「too + 形容詞 + to V.」的用法

　　　解　答：Kevin is too young to go to school.

　　句型分析：主詞 + be 動詞 + too + 形容詞 + to V.

　　　説　明：這題的意思是說「凱文年紀太小，沒辦法上學」，
　　　　　　　用 too…to V. 合併，表「太…以致於不~」。

8. I have a sister.

My sister's name is Jennifer.

I have _____ Jennifer.

　　重點結構：whose 的用法

　　　解　答：I have a sister whose name is Jennifer.

　　句型分析：I have a sister + whose + 名詞 + 動詞

　　　説　明：這題的意思是說「我有一個名叫珍妮佛的姊姊」，
　　　　　　　在合併時，用 whose 表示所有格，引導形容詞子
　　　　　　　句。

9. I like to eat peanut butter very much.

My brother doesn't like to eat peanut butter.

I like _____ peanut butter very much, _____ it.

　　重點結構：but 的用法

解　答：I like to eat peanut butter very much, but my brother doesn't like it.

句型分析：主詞 + 動詞 + but + 主詞 + 動詞

說　明：but 是對等連接詞，表示語氣上的轉折。

* peanut〔'pi,nʌt〕n. 花生
 butter〔'bʌtɚ〕n. 奶油
 peanut butter 花生醬

10. Bob is fixing his computer.
 Nancy helps him.
 Nancy helps ＿＿＿＿＿＿＿＿＿＿＿＿＿＿＿＿＿＿＿.

重點結構：「help + *sb.* + (to) V.」的用法

解　答：Nancy helps Bob (to) fix his computer.

句型分析：help + 受詞 + 不定詞或原形動詞

說　明：這題的意思是「南西幫巴伯修電腦」，help 的用法是接受詞後，須接不定詞，不定詞的 to 也可省略。

* fix〔fɪks〕v. 修理　　computer〔kəm'pjutɚ〕n. 電腦

第 11～15 題：重組

11. What ＿＿＿＿＿＿＿＿＿＿＿＿＿＿＿＿＿＿＿＿＿＿＿?
 Kelly / her / do / like / animals / and / mother

重點結構：「What + 複數名詞？」的用法

解　答：What animals do Kelly and her mother like?

句型分析：What + 複數名詞 + 助動詞 + 主詞 + 動詞？

説　　明：這題的意思是「凱莉和她媽媽喜歡什麼動物？」

* animal〔ˈænəml̩〕*n.* 動物

12. I ＿＿＿＿＿＿＿＿＿＿＿＿＿＿＿＿＿＿＿＿＿＿＿＿.

at all / orange / don't / juice / like

重點結構：「not…at all」的用法

解　　答：<u>I don't like orange juice at all.</u>

句型分析：主詞 + 助動詞的否定 + 動詞 + 受詞 + at all

説　　明：這題的意思是「我一點都不喜歡柳橙」，not…at
　　　　　all 表示「一點也不」，爲否定句的加強語氣。

* orange〔ˈɔrɪndʒ〕*n.* 柳橙
　juice〔dʒus〕*n.* 果汁

13. David ＿＿＿＿＿＿＿＿＿＿＿＿＿＿＿＿＿＿＿＿＿.

best / is / one / friends / my / of

重點結構：「one of + 所有格 + 複數名詞」的用法

解　　答：<u>David is one of my best friends.</u>

句型分析：主詞 + be 動詞 + one of + 所有格 + 複數名詞

説　　明：題目的意思是「大衛是我最好的朋友之一」，
　　　　　「～當中的一個」用「one of + 複數名詞」來
　　　　　表示。

14. Sandra _____.

earthquake / when / watching / the / happened / was / TV

　　重點結構：「主詞 + 動詞 + when 子句」的用法

　　解　答：Sandra was watching TV when the earthquake happened.

　　句型分析：主詞 + be 動詞 + 現在分詞 + when + 主詞 + 動詞

　　説　明：地震（earthquake）和發生（happened）連在一起，看（watching）和電視（TV）放在一起，重組成此句「當地震發生時，珊卓拉正在看電視」。

　　* earthquake〔'ɝθ,kwek〕n. 地震
　　happen〔'hæpən〕v. 發生

15. Please _____.

page / turn to / seven / number

　　重點結構：祈使句的用法

　　解　答：Please turn to page number seven.

　　句型分析：Please + 原形動詞

　　説　明：這題的意思是「請翻到第七頁」，用祈使句的句型，須以原形動詞開頭。

　　* turn〔tɝn〕v. 翻動　　page〔pedʒ〕n. 頁

第二部份：段落寫作

題目：上星期天，我們全家出遊到山上野餐（have a picnic）。
請根據以下的圖片寫一篇約 50 字的短文。

Last Sunday, my family and I drove to the mountains.
We had a picnic beside a lake. My father tried to catch some
fish in the lake. My mother cooked some food on a barbecue
while I was playing the guitar and singing songs. *Later on* we
all ate the food. We had a good time *last Sunday*.

上個星期日，我家人和我開車去山上。我們在湖旁邊野餐。我
父親嘗試抓一些湖中的魚。我母親烤了一些食物，而我彈吉他唱
歌。之後我們一起吃了食物。我們上個星期日有個愉快的時光。

drive〔draɪv〕v. 開車　　mountain〔ˈmaʊntn̩〕n. 山
picnic〔ˈpɪknɪk〕n. 野餐　　*have a picnic* 去野餐
beside〔bɪˈsaɪd〕prep. 在…旁邊　　lake〔lek〕n. 湖
try to + *V.* 試著要～　　catch〔kætʃ〕v. 捕捉
cook〔kʊk〕v. 烹煮　　barbecue〔ˈbɑrbɪˌkju〕n. 烤肉架
play the guitar 彈吉他　　*later on* 之後（= *later*）

口說能力測驗詳解

＊請在15秒內完成並唸出下列自我介紹的句子：

My seat number is ﹙複試座位號碼後5碼﹚, and my test
number is ﹙初試准考證號碼後5碼﹚.

I. 複誦

共五題。題目不印在試卷上，由耳機播出，
每題播出兩次，兩次之間大約有一至二秒
的間隔。聽完兩次後，請馬上複誦一次。

1. Make up your mind already! 快點下定決心！

2. Have you met him before? 你之前見過他嗎？

3. The bus will be here soon.
   公車很快要到了。

4. What did she say exactly?
   她到底說了什麼？

5. That's a lot of money.
   那是一大筆錢。

【註】 *make up one's mind* 下定決心
　　　already﹝ɔlˈrɛdɪ﹞*adv.*（用於強調語氣）快；可以
　　　exactly﹝ɪgˈzæktlɪ﹞*adv.* 正確地；精確地
　　　a lot of 很多

II. 朗讀句子與短文

共有五個句子及一篇短文，請先利用一分
鐘的時間閱讀試卷上的句子與短文，然後
在一分鐘內以正常的速度，清楚正確的朗讀一遍，閱讀時請不要
發出聲音。

One　　: Feel free to call me at 2209-3388.

隨時打電話 2209-3388 來找我。

Two　　: For the next two weeks, the store will stay open
until 10:00 p.m.

接下來的兩週，商店會開到晚上十點。

Three　: The manager is sick, so the store will be closed
tomorrow.

經理生病了，所以商店明天不營業。

Four　　: You've been here many times, haven't you?

你來過這好幾次了，不是嗎？

Five　　: The voice of the talking robot sounds like a real
person.

這會講話的機器人的聲音聽起來像真人。

【註】free〔fri〕*adj.* 自由的；隨意的
call〔kɔl〕*v.* 打電話給　　stay〔ste〕*v.* 保持
open〔'opən〕*adj.* 開放的；營業的
until〔ən'tɪl〕*prep.* 直到

p.m. 午後；下午 (= *post meridiem*)
manager〔'mænɪdʒɚ〕*n.* 經理
store〔stor〕*n.* 商店　　time〔taɪm〕*n.* 次數
robot〔'robət〕*n.* 機器人

Six　：Helen used to live in an old apartment, and there
was plenty of space for her outdoor plants. Now
she lives in a modern building. It's a much nicer
place, but there's no room for her plants. So she
had to ask her mother to take them.

海倫以前住在舊公寓裡，有很多空間給她戶外的植物。
現在她住在新式的建築物裡。這是更好的住所，但是沒
有空間放她的植物。所以她必須請她母親接收它們。

【註】*used to V.* 以前～　　old〔old〕*adj.* 舊的
apartment〔ə'partmənt〕*n.* 公寓
plenty of 很多　　space〔spes〕*n.* 空間
outdoor〔'aʊt,dor〕*adj.* 戶外的
plant〔plænt〕*n.* 植物
modern〔'madɚn〕*adj.* 現代的；新式的
building〔'bɪldɪŋ〕*n.* 建築物
much〔mʌtʃ〕*adv.* (修飾比較級) 非常
room〔rum〕*n.* 房間；空間

III. 回答問題

共七題。題目不印在試卷上，由耳機播出，
每題播出兩次，兩次之間大約有一至二秒的
間隔。聽完兩次後，請馬上回答。每題回答時間爲 15 秒，回答
時不一定要用完整的句子，請在作答時間內儘量的表達。

1. **Q**：How much do you study on weekends?
　　你週末讀多久的書？

　A：I study about eight hours on Saturdays and maybe five hours on Sundays.
　　我週六讀大約八小時，週日可能五小時。

　【註】weekend〔'wik'ɛnd〕*n.* 週末
　　　　hour〔aʊr〕*n.* 小時　　maybe〔'mebi〕*adv.* 或許；可能

2. **Q**：What beverage do you like best? Why?
　　你最喜歡什麼飲料？爲什麼？

　A：I like bubble tea best. Because it's tasty!
　　我最喜歡泡沫紅茶。因爲很好喝！

　【註】beverage〔'bɛvərɪdʒ〕*n.* 飲料
　　　　bubble〔'bʌbl〕*n.* 泡沫；氣泡
　　　　bubble tea 泡沫紅茶　　tasty〔'testɪ〕*adj.* 美味的

3. **Q**：How much exercise do you get? Is it enough for you?
　　你做多少運動？這對你而言足夠嗎？

　A：I get an hour of exercise per week. No, I think I need more.

我每週運動一小時。不，我覺得我需要更多。

【註】exercise〔'ɛksə͵saɪz〕 n. 運動

enough〔ə'nʌf〕 adj. 足夠的　　per〔pə〕 prep. 每…

4. **Q**：When was the last time you went to see a movie?
Did you like it?

你上一次去看電影是什麼時候？你喜歡嗎？

A：I saw a movie maybe a month ago. It was OK.

我大概一個月前看了電影。那電影還可以。

【註】*last time* 上一次　　 *see a movie* 看電影

5. **Q**：Do you ever visit with relatives? What do you do?

你曾和親戚閒聊嗎？你做些什麼？

A：I visit with relatives all the time. We usually eat.

我總是和親戚閒聊。我們通常會吃飯。

【註】ever〔'ɛvə〕 adv. 曾經　　 visit〔'vɪzɪt〕 v. 拜訪

visit with 閒談　　 relative〔'rɛlətɪv〕 n. 親戚

all the time 總是

usually〔'judʒuəlɪ〕 adv. 通常；一般

6. **Q**：You're shopping at the mall and you see your
favorite pop star. What will you do?

你在商場購物並看見你最喜愛的明星。你會做什麼？

A：Nothing. Maybe try to take a picture. I would be too
shy to approach her.

什麼都不會。可能試著照張相。我會太害羞不敢接近她。

【註】shop〔ʃɑp〕v. 購物　　mall〔mɔl〕n. 購物中心；商場
favorite〔'fevərɪt〕adj. 最喜愛的　　*pop star* 流行明星
take a picture 照相　　*too~to V.* 太~而無法
shy〔ʃaɪ〕adj. 害羞的　　approach〔ə'protʃ〕v. 接近

7. **Q**：You left your cell phone at the library, and you want
to know whether it has been found. Call the library
to find out.
你把手機遺留在圖書館了，而你想要知道是否有被找到。打
電話到圖書館看看。

A：Hello, my name is Dave. I left my cell phone there
not too long ago. Did anyone find it and turn it in?
哈囉，我是戴夫。我不久前把手機遺留在那裡了。有任何人
找到並歸還嗎？

【註】*cell phone* 手機　　library〔'laɪˌbrɛrɪ〕n. 圖書館
find out 發現；知道　　*turn in* 交付；歸還

＊請將下列自我介紹的句子再唸一遍：

My seat number is （複試座位號碼後5碼）, and my test
number is （初試准考證號碼後5碼）.

初級英語檢定複試測驗⑧詳解

寫作能力測驗詳解

第一部份：單句寫作

第1~5題：句子改寫

1. My boyfriend cooked me some spaghetti.

   My boyfriend ＿＿＿＿＿＿＿＿＿＿＿＿＿＿＿＿ me.

   > 重點結構：cook 的用法
   >
   > 解　答：My boyfriend cooked some spaghetti for me.
   >
   > 句型分析：cook + 直接受詞（物）+ for + 間接受詞（人）
   >
   > 說　明：「為某人煮東西」有兩種寫法：「cook + *sb.* + *sth.*」或「cook + *sth.* + for + *sb.*」，這題要改成第二種用法，先寫物（some spaghetti），再寫介系詞 for，再接人（me）。
   >
   > * spaghetti〔spə'gɛtɪ〕*n.* 義大利麵

2. Cartoons are interesting to most children.

   Most children are ＿＿＿＿＿＿＿＿＿＿＿＿＿＿ cartoons.

   > 重點結構：「be 動詞 + interested + in」的用法
   >
   > 解　答：Most children are interested in cartoons.
   >
   > 句型分析：主詞 + be 動詞 + interested + in + 受詞
   >
   > 說　明：動詞 interest「使感興趣」的形容詞有兩個，一個是現在分詞 interesting，一個是過去分詞 interested，其用法為：

$$\begin{cases} \text{事物} + \text{be 動詞} + \text{interesting} + \text{to} + \text{人} \\ \text{人} + \text{be 動詞} + \text{interested} + \text{in} + \text{事物} \end{cases}$$

本題的主詞是 Most children，故用形容詞

interested。

* cartoon〔kɑr'tun〕*n.* 卡通影片

3. Tina went to the swimming school.

　When ＿＿＿＿＿＿＿＿＿＿＿＿＿＿＿＿＿＿＿＿＿?

　　重點結構：過去式的 wh- 問句

　　　解　答：When did Tina go to the swimming school?

　　句型分析：When + did + 主詞 + 原形動詞？

　　說　　明：這一題應將過去式直述句改爲 wh- 問句，除了要加
　　　　　　　助動詞 did，還要記得助動詞後面的動詞，須用原
　　　　　　　形動詞，因此 went 要改成 go。

　　* *swimming school* 游泳訓練班

4. To keep it a secret may be a good idea.

　It ＿＿＿＿＿＿＿＿＿＿＿＿＿＿＿＿＿＿＿＿＿.

　　重點結構：以 It 爲虛主詞引導的句子

　　　解　答：It may be a good idea to keep it a secret.

　　句型分析：It + 助動詞 + 動詞 + 名詞 + 不定詞

　　說　　明：虛主詞 It 代替不定詞片語，不定詞片語 to keep
　　　　　　　it a secret 才是眞正的主詞，須置於句尾。

　　* keep〔kip〕*v.* 使停留在…狀態
　　　secret〔'sikrɪt〕*n.* 秘密　　*keep it a secret* 保密

5. The Greens bought that house last week.

That house _____ last week.

　重點結構：被動語態字序

　　解　答：<u>That house was bought by the Greens last</u>
　　　　　　<u>week.</u>

　句型分析：主詞 + be 動詞 + 過去分詞 + by + 受詞

　　說　明：被動語態的形式是「be 動詞 + 過去分詞」，
　　　　　　故動詞 bought 須改爲 was bought。

第 6～10 題：句子合併

6. I saw my brother in the living room.

My brother was watching TV.

I saw _____ in the living room.

　重點結構：see 的用法

　　解　答：<u>I saw my brother watch TV in the living room.</u>
　　或　　　<u>I saw my brother watching TV in the living</u>
　　　　　　<u>room.</u>

　句型分析：主詞 + 動詞 + 受詞 + 原形動詞或現在分詞

　　說　明：see 的用法：

　　　　　　$\begin{cases} \text{see} + 受詞 + 原形動詞（表主動）\\ \text{see} + 受詞 + 現在分詞（表主動進行）\end{cases}$

7. This postcard is pretty.

That postcard is pretty.

This postcard _____ as that postcard.

重點結構：「as…as～」的用法

解　　答：<u>This postcard is as pretty as that postcard.</u>

句型分析：主詞 + be 動詞 + as + 形容詞 + as + 受詞

説　　明：這題是說這兩張照片都很漂亮，用「as…as～」
　　　　　來連接兩句，表「和～一樣…」。

* postcard〔'post,kɑrd〕n. 明信片
　 pretty〔'prɪtɪ〕adj. 漂亮的

8. We have to walk fast.

We want to catch the train.

Walk fast, or ＿＿＿＿＿＿ will not ＿＿＿＿＿＿＿＿＿.

重點結構：or 的用法

解　　答：<u>Walk fast, or we will not catch the train.</u>

句型分析：原形動詞, or + 主詞 + 動詞

説　　明：這題的意思是說「走快點，不然我們就趕不上火車
　　　　　了」，連接詞 or 表「否則」。

* catch〔kætʃ〕v. 趕上

9. I have been reading a novel.

I just finished it two days ago.

I just finished ＿＿＿＿＿＿＿＿＿＿＿＿＿＿＿.

重點結構：finish 的用法

解　　答：<u>I just finished (reading) a novel two days ago.</u>

句型分析：主詞 + 動詞 + (動)名詞 + 時間副詞

說　明：finish（完成）的用法是後面接名詞或動名詞做受
詞，故有兩種寫法：finished a novel 或 finished
reading a novel。

＊ novel〔ˋnɑvḷ〕 n. 小說

10. My dog is smart.
My dog is cute.
My dog is not only ＿＿＿＿＿＿＿＿＿＿＿＿＿＿＿＿＿＿＿.

重點結構：「not only…but (also)～」的用法
解　答：My dog is not only smart but (also) cute.
句型分析：主詞＋be 動詞＋not only＋形容詞＋but (also)
＋形容詞
說　明：這題的意思是說「我的小狗既聰明又可愛」，
用「not only…but (also)～」來連接兩句，
表「不但～而且…」。

第 11～15 題：重組

11. Do you know ＿＿＿＿＿＿＿＿＿＿＿＿＿＿＿＿＿＿＿＿？
when / plane / take / the / off / will

重點結構：「Do you know＋when＋主詞＋動詞」的用法
解　答：Do you know when the plane will take off?
句型分析：Do you know＋疑問詞＋主詞＋動詞？
說　明：when 引導名詞子句，做動詞 know 的受詞。

＊ plane〔plen〕 n. 飛機　　*take off* 起飛

12. Which ＿＿＿＿＿＿＿＿＿＿＿＿＿＿＿＿, black or white?

　　like / color / you / better / do

　　　重點結構：wh- 問句的用法

　　　　解　答：Which color do you like better, black or white?

　　　句型分析：Which + 名詞 + 助動詞 + 主詞 + 動詞？

　　　　説　明：本句的意思是「你比較喜歡哪一個顏色，黑色或白色？」即問句的形式，先寫助動詞，再寫主詞。

　　　＊ color〔ˈkʌlɚ〕 n. 顏色

13. It's ＿＿＿＿＿＿＿＿＿＿＿＿＿＿＿＿＿＿＿＿＿＿.

　　impossible / near / to find / a / almost / parking space /
　　our school

　　　重點結構：以 It 為虛主詞引導的句子

　　　　解　答：It's almost impossible to find a parking space near our school.

　　　句型分析：It's + 形容詞 + 不定詞

　　　　説　明：虛主詞 It 代替不定詞片語，不定詞片語 to find a parking space near our school 才是真正的主詞，須置於句尾。副詞 almost 修飾形容詞 impossible。

　　　＊ almost〔ˈɔlˌmost〕 adv. 幾乎
　　　　impossible〔ɪmˈpɑsəbl̩〕 adj. 不可能的
　　　　space〔spes〕 n. 空位
　　　　parking space 停車位
　　　　near〔nɪr〕 prep. 在…附近

14. How _____?

　　you / would / your / like / steak

　　　重點結構：wh- 問句的用法

　　　解　答：<u>How would you like your steak?</u>

　　　句型分析：How + 助動詞 + 主詞 + 動詞 ?

　　　說　明：本句是問「你的牛排要幾分熟？」即問句的形式，

　　　　　　　先寫助動詞，再寫主詞。

　　　* steak〔stek〕n. 牛排

15. Robert _____.

　　come / this evening / will / to / visit / us

　　　重點結構：「主詞 + 助動詞+ 動詞」的用法

　　　解　答：<u>Robert will come to visit us this evening.</u>

　　　句型分析：主詞 + 助動詞 + 動詞

　　　說　明：這題有三個動詞 come、will 和 visit，助動詞 will

　　　　　　　須擺在最前面，後面接原形動詞 come，visit 前面

　　　　　　　加 to，形成不定詞，表目的，故本句的意思是「羅

　　　　　　　伯特今晚將來拜訪我們」。

　　　* visit〔'vɪzɪt〕v. 拜訪

第二部份：段落寫作

題目：昨天是中秋節（Mid-Autumn Festival）。請根據以下的圖
　　　片寫一篇約 50 字的短文。

Yesterday was the Mid-Autumn Festival. My family
and I had a barbecue outside. We ate meat and bread. *After*
we ate, my mother told us a story. She told us about Chang
O, the lady in the moon. She drank a magical drink, and
then flew to the moon. She still lives there.

After the story, we looked at the moon. The moon was
full. We ate a lot of moon cakes. We all had a good time
last night.

　　昨天是中秋節。我的家人和我在外面烤肉。我們吃肉和麵包。
吃完之後，我母親告訴我們一個故事。她跟我們說關於嫦娥，也就
是月娘的事情。她喝了一個神奇的酒，然後就飛向了月亮。她依然
住在那裡。

　　聽完故事後，我們看著月亮。是滿月。我們吃了很多月餅。我
們昨晚有個愉快的時光。

mid- 〔 mɪd 〕中間的（用於複合字）　　autumn 〔ˋɔtəm〕 *n.* 秋天
festival 〔ˋfɛstəvḷ〕 *n.* 節日　　*Mid-Autumn Festival*　中秋節
outside 〔ˋautˋsaɪd〕 *adv.* 在戶外　　bread 〔 brɛd 〕 *n.* 麵包
Chang O　嫦娥　　lady 〔ˋledɪ〕 *n.* 女士；小姐
moon 〔 mun 〕 *n.* 月亮
magical 〔ˋmædʒɪkḷ〕 *adj.* 有魔力的；神奇的
drink 〔 drɪŋk 〕 *n.* 飲料；酒類
fly 〔 flaɪ 〕 *v.* 飛【三態變化為：fly-flew-flown】
look at　看　　full 〔 fʊl 〕 *adj.* 滿月的
moon cake　月餅　　*have a good time*　玩得愉快

口說能力測驗詳解

*請在15秒內完成並唸出下列自我介紹的句子：

My seat number is （複試座位號碼後5碼）, and my test
number is （初試准考證號碼後5碼）.

I. 複誦

共五題。題目不印在試卷上，由耳機播出，
每題播出兩次，兩次之間大約有一至二秒
的間隔。聽完兩次後，請馬上複誦一次。

1. How could you do that? 你怎麼可以那麼做？

2. So the book costs fifty dollars? 所以這本書要五十元？

3. Close the door. It's cold outside.
   關門。外面很冷。

4. I haven't seen her since Christmas.
   自從聖誕節之後我就沒看過她了。

5. He's going to be in Taichung next week, staying at the
   Park Hotel.
   他下星期會在台中，住在公園飯店。

【註】 cost〔kɔst〕v. 花費　　outside〔'aʊt'saɪd〕adv. 外面
　　　 since〔sɪns〕prep. 自從
　　　 Christmas〔'krɪsməs〕n. 聖誕節

II. 朗讀句子與短文

共有五個句子及一篇短文，請先利用一分
鐘的時間閱讀試卷上的句子與短文，然後
在一分鐘內以正常的速度，清楚正確的朗讀一遍，閱讀時請不要
發出聲音。

One　： We're going to the 8:00 show.

我們要去八點的表演。

Two　： Why don't you ride your bike to school?

你何不騎腳踏車去學校？

Three ： I'll need to see some identification before I let you
in the building.

我需要看身份證件才能讓你進這棟建築物。

Four　： There will be a slight delay of approximately 20
minutes.

會有大約二十分鐘的延遲。

Five　： She's a big dog, but she's really friendly and
well-behaved.

牠是一隻大狗，但是牠真的很友善且乖巧。

【註】 show〔ʃo〕n. 表演　　ride〔raɪd〕v. 騎
bicycle〔'baɪˌsɪkḷ〕n. 腳踏車
identification〔aɪˌdɛntəfə'keʃən〕n. 身份證明
building〔'bɪldɪŋ〕n. 建築物　　slight〔slaɪt〕adj. 些許的

delay〔dɪ'le〕*n.* 延遲
approximately〔ə'prɑksəmɪtlɪ〕*adv.* 大約
friendly〔'frɛndlɪ〕*adj.* 友善的
well-behaved〔'wɛlbɪ'hevd〕*adj.* 行為端正的;循規蹈矩的

Six : Hi, this is Alice. I'm calling about Tom's birthday
party. I'm bringing a cake and Greg is bringing
some drinks. Could you help with the decorations?
Maybe you could make a big banner or poster.

嗨,我是愛麗斯。我打電話是要問關於湯姆的生日派對。
我帶了蛋糕,而葛雷格帶一些飲料。你可以幫忙佈置嗎?
或許你可以做個大的橫幅或是海報。

【註】 *this is* (用於講電話)我是   *birthday party* 生日派對
cake〔kek〕*n.* 蛋糕   drink〔drɪŋk〕*n.* 飲料
help〔hɛlp〕*v.* 幫助   decoration〔ˌdɛkə'reʃən〕*n.* 佈置
maybe〔'mebi〕*adv.* 或許;可能
banner〔'bænɚ〕*n.* 橫幅標語;旗幟
poster〔'postɚ〕*n.* 海報

III. 回答問題

共七題。題目不印在試卷上，由耳機播出，
每題播出兩次，兩次之間大約有一至二秒的
間隔。聽完兩次後，請馬上回答。每題回答時間為 15 秒，回答
時不一定要用完整的句子，請在作答時間內儘量的表達。

1. **Q**: Do you prefer coffee, tea, or something else?

   你偏好咖啡、茶，還是其他的？

   A: I like coffee and tea, but I prefer fresh fruit juice.

   我喜歡咖啡和茶，但是我偏好新鮮果汁。

   【註】prefer〔prɪˋfɝ〕v. 偏好；比較喜歡
   coffee〔ˋkɔfɪ〕n. 咖啡　　fresh〔frɛʃ〕adj. 新鮮的
   fruit juice 果汁

2. **Q**: Are you a light sleeper?　Are you easily wakened by loud noises?

   你是淺眠的人嗎？你容易被噪音吵醒嗎？

   A: No, I'm a heavy sleeper.　I can sleep through a tornado.

   不，我睡得很沈。龍捲風來我也可以沈睡不醒。

   【註】light〔laɪt〕adj. 輕的；淺的　　***light sleeper*** 淺眠的人
   easily〔ˋizɪlɪ〕adv. 容易地　　waken〔ˋwekən〕v. 叫醒
   loud〔laʊd〕adj. 大聲的　　noise〔nɔɪz〕n. 噪音
   heavy sleeper 熟睡的人
   sleep through 在…中沈睡不醒
   tornado〔tɔrˋnedo〕n. 龍捲風

3. **Q**：How long does it take you to get to school?

去學校要花你多少時間？

A：It takes me about 15 minutes to get to school.

去學校要花我大約十五分鐘。

【註】take〔tek〕*v.* 花（時間）　　***get to*** 到達

4. **Q**：When was the last time you took a taxi? Where did you go?

你上一次搭計程車是什麼時候？你去哪裡？

A：The last time I took a taxi was maybe a week ago. We went to Taipei 101.

我上一次搭計程車可能是一個星期之前。我們去台北 101。

【註】***last time*** 上一次　　taxi〔'tæksɪ〕*n.* 計程車

5. **Q**：What kind of music do you like? Why?

你喜歡哪種音樂？爲什麼？

A：I like all kinds of music, but my favorite is hip-hop. I like it because it usually has a nice beat and some of the sounds are cool.

我喜歡各種音樂，但是我最喜愛的是嘻哈音樂。我喜歡它是因爲它通常有很棒的節拍，而且有些聲音很酷。

【註】kind〔kaɪnd〕*n.* 種類　　music〔'mjuzɪk〕*n.* 音樂
favorite〔'fevərɪt〕*adj.* 最喜愛的
hip-hop〔'hɪp,hɑp〕*n.* 嘻哈音樂【20世紀80年代開始流行
　　於美國黑人青年之間，以說唱樂、塗鴉藝術爲特徵】
beat〔bit〕*n.* 節拍　　cool〔kul〕*adj.* 酷的

6. **Q** : Did you take the bus today? How did you get here?

   你今天有搭公車嗎？你如何到這裡的？

   A : Yes, I took a bus today. I took the 235 bus to get here.

   有的，我今天搭公車。我搭 235 號公車到這裡。

   【註】bus〔bʌs〕*n.* 公車

7. **Q** : Some older boys are picking on a younger boy in the cafeteria. What will you do?

   自助餐廳裡，有些年長的男孩正在刁難一位年幼的男孩。
   你會做什麼？

   A : I will go over there and stand up for the boy who is being picked on. If the bullies want to fight somebody, they can fight me.

   我會走過去並幫助被刁難的男孩。如果惡霸想要找人打架，
   他們可以和我打。

   【註】*pick on* 找麻煩；刁難
   cafeteria〔͵kæfə'tɪrɪə〕*n.* 自助餐廳
   stand up for 支持；捍衛
   bully〔'bulɪ〕*n.* 惡霸；霸凌者
   fight〔faɪt〕*v.* 與…作戰；和…打架

*請將下列自我介紹的句子再唸一遍：

My seat number is （複試座位號碼後 5 碼）, and my test
number is （初試准考證號碼後 5 碼）.

初級英語檢定複試測驗 ⑨ 詳解

寫作能力測驗詳解

第一部份：單句寫作

第 1～5 題：句子改寫

1. I asked Tina, "Could you open the window?"

   I asked Tina whether _____.

   重點結構：以 whether 引導名詞子句的用法

   解　答：<u>I asked Tina whether she could open the window.</u>

   句型分析：I asked Tina + whether + 主詞 + 動詞

   說　明：Could you open the window? 是直接問句，現在要放在 whether（是否）後面，做為 I asked Tina 的受詞，即名詞子句（間接問句）「連接詞 + 主詞 + 動詞」的形式，在 I asked Tina 後面接 whether you could open the window，並把問號改成句點。

   * whether〔ˈhwɛðɚ〕conj. 是否

2. Sally is shorter than all the other students in her class.

   Sally _____ shortest _____ in her class.

   重點結構：比較級表達最高級的用法

解　答：<u>Sally is the shortest student in her class.</u>

句型分析：主詞 + be 動詞 + the + 形容詞最高級 + 名詞

説　明：題目的意思是「莎莉比她班上的其他學生矮」，換句話說，「莎莉是她班上最矮的學生」，可以用最高級表達，在 shortest 之前須加定冠詞 the，並把 students 改為單數名詞 student。

3. Tim didn't go to school because he didn't feel well.

Tim _____, so _____.

重點結構：so 的用法

解　答：<u>Tim didn't feel well, so he didn't go to school.</u>

句型分析：主詞 + 動詞 + so + 主詞 + 動詞

説　明：連接詞 because（因為）和 so（所以）的比較：

結果 + because + 原因
原因 + so + 結果

＊ well〔wɛl〕*adj.* 身體健康的

4. Jane didn't hand in her report on time.

Why _____?

重點結構：wh- 問句的用法

解　答：<u>Why didn't Jane hand in her report on time?</u>

句型分析：Why + didn't + 主詞 + 原形動詞？

説　明：這一題應將過去式的否定直述句改為 wh- 問句，助動詞 didn't 與主詞 Jane 倒裝即可。

* ***hand in*** 繳交　　report〔rɪ'port〕*n.* 報告
  on time 準時

5. Our teacher made this cake.

   This cake ＿＿＿＿＿＿＿＿＿＿＿＿＿＿ our teacher.

   重點結構：被動語態字序

   　解　答：<u>This cake was made by our teacher.</u>

   句型分析：主詞 + be 動詞 + 過去分詞 + by + 受詞

   　說　明：被動語態的形式是「be 動詞 + 過去分詞」，
   故動詞 made 須改爲 was made。

第 6～10 題：句子合併

6. Kevin has a backpack.

   The backpack is black.

   Kevin ＿＿＿＿＿＿＿＿＿＿＿＿＿＿ backpack.

   重點結構：形容詞與名詞字序

   　解　答：<u>Kevin has a black backpack.</u>

   句型分析：主詞 + 動詞 + 形容詞 + 名詞

   　說　明：表達顏色的形容詞，放在要修飾的名詞之前。

   * backpack〔'bæk,pæk〕*n.* 背包

7. Where are they going to?

   I'd like to know.

   I'd like to know where ＿＿＿＿＿＿＿＿＿＿＿.

重點結構：間接問句做名詞子句

解　答：<u>I'd like to know where they are going to.</u>

句型分析：I'd like to know + where + 主詞 + 動詞

說　明：在 wh- 問句前加 I'd like to know，形成間接問句，即「疑問詞 + 主詞 + 動詞」的形式，因此必須把動詞 are going to 放在最後面，並把問號改成句點。

8. Little Wendy can't sleep.

She needs to hold her blanket.

Little Wendy _____ without _____.

重點結構：without 的用法

解　答：<u>Little Wendy can't sleep without (holding) her blanket.</u>

句型分析：主詞 + 動詞 + without + (動) 名詞

說　明：without (沒有) 為介系詞，後面須接名詞或動名詞，故可接 her blanket 或 holding her blanket。

* hold〔hold〕v. 抱著　　blanket〔'blæŋkɪt〕n. 毛毯

9. I have a computer.

My computer is new and expensive.

I have _____ which _____.

重點結構：由 which 引導的形容詞子句

解　答：<u>I have a computer which is new and expensive.</u>

句型分析：I have a computer + which + 動詞

　説　明：句意是「我有一台電腦，這台電腦既新穎又昂貴。」
　　　　　在合併兩句時，用 which 代替先行詞 a computer，
　　　　　引導形容詞子句，在子句中做主詞。

* computer〔kəm'pjutɚ〕 n. 電腦
　expensive〔ɪk'spɛnsɪv〕 adj. 昂貴的

10. My mother is here.
　　My father is here, too.
　　Both ＿＿＿＿＿ and ＿＿＿＿＿＿＿＿＿.

　重點結構：both A and B 的用法

　　解　答：<u>Both my mother and my father are here.</u>

　句型分析：Both + 名詞 + and + 名詞 + 動詞

　　説　明：題意是「我母親跟我父親兩人都在這裡。」用
　　　　　「both…and～」合併兩個主詞，表「…和～
　　　　　兩者都」。

第 11～15 題：重組

11. Peter ＿＿＿＿＿＿＿＿＿＿＿＿＿＿＿＿＿＿.
　　understanding / what / has / the child / is saying / trouble

　重點結構：「have trouble + V-ing」的用法

　　解　答：<u>Peter has trouble understanding what the child</u>
　　　　　<u>is saying.</u>

句型分析：主詞 + have trouble + 動名詞

説　明：have trouble + V-ing 表「做…有困難」，have trouble 後面省略介系詞 in，故後面加動名詞。

12. I _____.

get up / in / at / used to / the morning / five o'clock

重點結構：「used to + 原形 V.」的用法

解　答：<u>I used to get up at five o'clock in the morning.</u>

句型分析：主詞 + used to + 原形動詞

説　明：used to 表「以前」，整句的意思是說「我以前習慣早上五點鐘起床。」

13. Keep _____!

or / get / quiet / out

重點結構：or 的用法

解　答：<u>Keep quiet or get out!</u>

句型分析：原形動詞，or + 主詞 + 動詞

説　明：這題的意思是說「安靜點，不然就出去！」，連接詞 or 表「否則」。

* keep〔kip〕v. 保持在…狀態　　quiet〔'kwaɪət〕adj. 安靜的
get out 出去

14. James _____.

looking for / for / a / house / has / a while / new / been

重點結構：現在完成進行式字序

解　答：James has been looking for a new house for a while.

句型分析：主詞 + have/has + been + 現在分詞 + for a while

説　明：一般現在完成進行式的結構是「主詞 + have/has + 現在分詞」，而 for a while，表「（持續）一段時間」，此時間片語須置於句尾。

* **look for** 尋找
while〔hwaɪl〕*n.* 一會兒；一段時間

15. Gary _____.

as long as / is not / will / raining / jog / it

重點結構：as long as 的用法

解　答：Gary will jog as long as it is not raining.

句型分析：主詞 + 動詞 + as long as + 主詞 + 動詞

説　明：as long as 表「只要」，爲連接詞片語，引導副詞子句，即完整的主詞加動詞，本題的意思是「蓋瑞會去慢跑，只要沒有下雨的話」。

* jog〔dʒɑg〕*v.* 慢跑

第二部份：段落寫作

題目： 現在正是暑假時期，下面是你每天的活動。請根據以下的圖
　　　 片寫一篇約 50 字的短文。

I am very busy this summer vacation. ***In the morning*** I go to a swim class. I like to play with my friends in the water. ***In the afternoon*** I go to my English class. We play games and sing English songs. ***In the evening*** I eat dinner with my parents. I tell them what I did that day. Summer vacation is a lot of fun.

我這個暑假很忙。早上我去上游泳課。我喜歡和朋友玩水。下午我去上英文課。我們玩遊戲並唱英文歌。傍晚我和父母吃晚餐。我告訴他們我那天做的事。暑假很有趣。

> *summer vacation*　暑假
> *a swim class*　游泳課
> *be a lot of fun*　很有趣

口説能力測驗詳解

*請在15秒內完成並唸出下列自我介紹的句子：

My seat number is （複試座位號碼後5碼）, and my test
number is （初試准考證號碼後5碼）.

I. 複誦

共五題。題目不印在試卷上，由耳機播出，
每題播出兩次，兩次之間大約有一至二秒
的間隔。聽完兩次後，請馬上複誦一次。

1. Fred is always late. 弗雷德總是遲到。

2. Here comes that guy you don't like.
   你不喜歡的人來了。

3. Welcome, shoppers.
   顧客您好，歡迎光臨。

4. Where did you last see the wallet?
   你最近在哪裡看到皮夾？

5. I'll call you when I get home.
   我到家會打電話給你。

【註】 late〔let〕adj. 遲到的　　guy〔gaɪ〕n. 人
　　　 welcome〔ˋwɛlkəm〕interj. 歡迎光臨
　　　 shopper〔ˋʃɑpɚ〕n. 購物者　　last〔læst〕adv. 最近；上次
　　　 wallet〔ˋwɑlɪt〕n. 皮夾　　call〔kɔl〕v. 打電話給

II. 朗讀句子與短文

共有五個句子及一篇短文，請先利用一分
鐘的時間閱讀試卷上的句子與短文，然後

在一分鐘內以正常的速度，清楚正確的朗讀一遍，閱讀時請不要
發出聲音。

One　：　What an exciting race! The fans are going crazy!

多麼刺激的比賽呀！粉絲們都瘋了！

Two　：　My brother is studying in Texas.

我哥哥正在德克薩斯州讀書。

Three　：　Most students go home during the winter break.

大部分的學生在寒假回家。

Four　：　When Mr. Carlson got to the office, the door was
locked and he did not have a key.

當卡爾森先生到辦公室時，門是鎖著，而他沒有鑰匙。

Five　：　You'd better review this information right now, or
you won't remember it for the exam.

你最好現在複習這資料，不然你在考試會想不起來。

【註】exciting〔ɪk'saɪtɪŋ〕*adj.* 令人興奮的；刺激的
　　　race〔res〕*n.* 比賽　　　fan〔fæn〕*n.* 迷
　　　go crazy 發瘋　　　Texas〔'tɛksəs〕*n.* 德克薩斯州
　　　break〔brek〕*n.* 休假　　　***get to*** 到達
　　　office〔'ɔfɪs〕*n.* 辦公室　　　lock〔lɑk〕*v.* 鎖
　　　key〔ki〕*n.* 鑰匙　　　***had better V.*** 最好～

review〔rɪ'vju〕v. 複習；再考量
information〔ˌɪnfə'meʃən〕n. 資訊；知識
right now 現在

Six　：Yesterday was Peter's birthday.　To celebrate, he invited some of his friends to have lunch at his favorite restaurant.　Everyone had a good time. When they finished eating, Peter paid the bill.

昨天是彼得的生日。為了慶祝，他邀請一些朋友在他最愛的餐廳吃午餐。每個人都玩得很愉快。當他們吃完後，彼得付帳。

【註】celebrate〔'sɛlə,bret〕v. 慶祝　　invite〔ɪn'vaɪt〕v. 邀請
have〔hæv〕v. 吃　　lunch〔lʌntʃ〕n. 午餐
favorite〔'fevərɪt〕adj. 最喜歡的
restaurant〔'rɛstərənt〕n. 餐廳
have a good time 玩得愉快　　finish〔'fɪnɪʃ〕v. 完成
paid〔ped〕v. 支付【pay 的過去式】
bill〔bɪl〕n. 帳單

III. 回答問題

共七題。題目不印在試卷上，由耳機播出，
每題播出兩次，兩次之間大約有一至二秒的
間隔。聽完兩次後，請馬上回答。每題回答時間為 15 秒，回答
時不一定要用完整的句子，請在作答時間內儘量的表達。

1. **Q**：When was the last time your family went out together?
   你上一次和家人一起外出是什麼時候？

   A：My family went out for brunch together last Sunday.
   我們一家上星期日一起出去吃早午餐。

   【註】*last time* 上一次 *go out* 外出
   brunch〔brʌntʃ〕*n.* 早午餐

2. **Q**：How often do you wash your clothes or how do they
   get clean? 你多久洗一次衣服，或是它們如何清理乾淨？

   A：I do my laundry about every two weeks at the
   Laundromat on Tonghua Street.
   我每兩週在通化街的自助洗衣店洗一次衣服。

   【註】*how often* 多常；多久一次 clothes〔kloz〕*n. pl.* 衣服
   get〔gɛt〕*v.* 變得 clean〔klin〕*adj.* 乾淨的
   laundry〔ˈlɔndrɪ〕*n.* 待洗的衣物
   do the laundry 洗衣服
   Laundromat〔ˈlɔndrəˌmæt〕*n.*（商標名）自助洗衣店

3. **Q**：How many pairs of shoes have you bought this year?
   你今年買了幾雙鞋子？

   A：I haven't bought any shoes this year. It's only January
   3! 我今年沒買任何鞋了，現在才一月三日。

【註】pair〔pɛr〕*n.* 一雙
bought〔bɔt〕*v.* 買【buy 的過去式】

4. **Q** : If someone invites you to dinner but you don't want to go, how can you politely refuse? 如果有人邀請你去吃晚餐，但是你不想要去，你會如何禮貌地拒絕？

A : I would say thank you very much for your offer, but I have plans. Maybe next time. 我會說非常謝謝你的提議，但是我有計畫了。或許下一次吧。

【註】invite〔ɪn'vaɪt〕*v.* 邀請　　dinner〔'dɪnɚ〕*n.* 晚餐
politely〔pə'laɪtlɪ〕*adv.* 有禮貌地
refuse〔rɪ'fjuz〕*v.* 拒絕　　offer〔'ɔfɚ〕*n.* 提議
plan〔plæn〕*n.* 計畫　　***next time*** 下一次

5. **Q** : Do you watch your weight? What could a person do to lose weight?
你有注意你的體重嗎？一個人可以做什麼來減重？

A : No, I don't watch my weight. A person could probably lose weight by eating a reasonable diet and getting some exercise. 不，我不注意我的體重。一個人可能可以靠合理的飲食和做些運動來減重。

【註】watch〔watʃ〕*v.* 注意　　weight〔wet〕*n.* 體重
lose weight 減重　　probably〔'prabəblɪ〕*adv.* 可能
reasonable〔'riznəbḷ〕*adj.* 合理的
diet〔'daɪət〕*n.* 飲食　　exercise〔'ɛksɚ͵saɪz〕*n.* 運動

6. **Q** : What is your ideal job? Please explain.
你理想的工作是什麼？請解釋。

A： My dream job is to be an architect. I've always been interested in designing and building things. Plus, I'm good at math and I have decent drafting skills.

我夢想的職業是當建築師。我一直對設計和建設東西有興趣。此外,我是數學很好,而且我的製圖技術還不錯。

【註】ideal〔aɪˈdiəl〕*adj.* 理想的　　job〔dʒab〕*n.* 工作
explain〔ɪkˈsplen〕*v.* 解釋
dream job 夢想職業　　architect〔ˈarkə,tɛkt〕*n.* 建築師
be interested in 對…感興趣　　design〔dɪˈzaɪn〕*v.* 設計
plus〔plʌs〕*adv.* 此外 (= *besides*)
be good at 擅長　　math〔mæθ〕*n.* 數學
decent〔ˈdisn̩t〕*adj.* 好的;不錯的
draft〔ˈdræftɪŋ〕*adj.* 製圖的　　skill〔skɪl〕*n.* 技術

7. **Q：** You hear that a school near your home is offering English courses at night. Call the school and ask a few questions. 你聽到在你家附近的學校正在提供夜間英語課程。打電話給該校並問一些問題。

A： Hey, I hear you have English classes. When are the classes? How much do they cost? What will we learn?

嘿,我聽到你們有英語課。什麼時候有課?費用是多少?我們會學些什麼?

【註】offer〔ˈɔfɚ〕*v.* 提供　　course〔kors〕*n.* 課程
a few 一些　　class〔klæs〕*n.* 講課
cost〔kɔst〕*v.* 花費

＊請將下列自我介紹的句子再唸一遍:

My seat number is （複試座位號碼後 5 碼）, and my test number is （初試准考證號碼後 5 碼）.

初級英語檢定複試測驗⑩詳解

寫作能力測驗詳解

第一部份：單句寫作

第1~5題：句子改寫

1. How much money does Ellen have?

   I'm not sure how much _____.

   重點結構：間接問句做名詞子句

   解　答：<u>I'm not sure how much money Ellen has.</u>

   句型分析：I'm not sure + how much money + 主詞 + 動詞

   說　明：在 wh- 問句前加 I'm not sure，須改為間接問
   句，即「疑問詞 + 主詞 + 動詞」的形式，又因
   主詞 Ellen 為第三人稱單數，have 須改為 has，
   並把問號改成句點。

   * sure〔ʃur〕*adj.* 確定的

2. Would you not smoke here?

   I don't want _____.

   重點結構：want 的用法

   解　答：<u>I don't want you to smoke here.</u>

   句型分析：主詞 + want + 受詞 + to V.

   說　明：Would you not smoke here?「你可不可以不要在
   這裡抽煙？」為婉轉的請求，實際上就是希望對方

　　　　　　　　　不要抽煙，用 want（想要）改寫，接受詞後，須接
　　　　　　　　　不定詞。

3. Taipei is bigger than any other city in Taiwan.

   Taipei _____ biggest _____ in Taiwan.

　　重點結構：比較級表達最高級的用法

　　解　　答：<u>Taipei is the biggest city in Taiwan.</u>

　　句型分析：主詞＋be 動詞＋the＋形容詞最高級＋名詞

　　說　　明：題目的意思是「台北比台灣其他任何的城市都大」，
　　　　　　　換句話說，「台北是台灣最大的城市。」可以用最
　　　　　　　高級表達，在 biggest 之前須加定冠詞 the，並接單
　　　　　　　數名詞 city。

4. I will never ride a roller coaster again!

   Never _____.

　　重點結構：Never 置於句首的用法

　　解　　答：<u>Never will I ride a roller coaster again!</u>

　　或　　　　<u>Never again will I ride a roller coaster!</u>

　　句型分析：Never＋助動詞＋主詞＋原形動詞

　　說　　明：never（絕不）為否定副詞，置於句首為加強語氣
　　　　　　　的用法，其後的主詞與動詞須倒裝。

　　* ride〔raɪd〕v. 乘坐　　***roller coaster*** 雲霄飛車

5. Rose felt sleepy, so she went to bed early.

   Rose _____ because_____.

重點結構：because 的用法

解　　答：<u>Rose went to bed early because she felt sleepy.</u>

句型分析：主詞 + 動詞 + because + 主詞 + 動詞

說　　明：連接詞 so（所以）和 because（因為）的比較：

$\left\{\begin{array}{l} \text{原因} + \text{so} + \text{結果} \\ \text{結果} + \text{because} + \text{原因} \end{array}\right.$

* sleepy〔'slipɪ〕*adj.* 想睡的

第 6～10 題：句子合併

6. I enjoyed the movie.
   We saw it last Friday.
   I enjoyed the movie ＿＿＿＿＿＿＿＿＿＿ last Friday.

重點結構：形容詞子句的用法

解　　答：<u>I enjoyed the movie which we saw last Friday.</u>

或　　　<u>I enjoyed the movie that we saw last Friday.</u>

或　　　<u>I enjoyed the movie we saw last Friday.</u>

句型分析：I enjoyed the movie +（關係代名詞）+ 主詞 + 動詞

說　　明：句意是「我喜歡上星期五看的那一部電影」，在
　　　　　合併兩句時，可用 which 或 that 代替先行詞 the
　　　　　movie，又因關係代名詞在引導的形容詞子句中，
　　　　　做動詞 saw 的受詞，故可省略不寫。

7. Sylvia is very friendly.
   Everyone in the office likes to talk to her.
   Sylvia is so ＿＿＿＿＿＿＿＿＿＿＿＿＿＿＿＿＿.

重點結構：「so + 形容詞 + that 子句」的用法

解　答：Sylvia is so friendly that everyone in the office likes to talk to her.

句型分析：主詞 + be 動詞 + so + 形容詞 + that + 主詞 + 動詞

説　明：這題的意思是說「席薇亞人很友善，所以辦公室裡的每個人都喜歡和她說話」，合併兩句時，用「so…that~」，表「如此…以致於~」。

＊ friendly〔'frɛndlɪ〕 adj. 友善的　　office〔'ɔfɪs〕 n. 辦公室

8. Heavy traffic wastes people's time.
Heavy traffic also produces serious air pollution.
Heavy traffic not only _____.

重點結構：「not only…but (also)~」的用法

解　答：Heavy traffic not only wastes people's time but (also) produces serious air pollution.

句型分析：主詞 + not only + 動詞 + but (also) + 動詞

説　明：這題的意思是說「交通擁擠，不僅浪費人們的時間，而且也製造嚴重的空氣污染」，合併兩句時，用「not only…but (also)~」表「不僅…，而且~」。

＊ heavy〔'hɛvɪ〕 adj. 大量的；擁擠的　　waste〔west〕 v. 浪費
produce〔prə'djus〕 v. 製造　　serious〔'sɪrɪəs〕 adj. 嚴重的
air〔ɛr〕 n. 空氣　　pollution〔pə'luʃən〕 n. 污染

9. Vivian studied for three hours.
Then she went out to get some sunshine.
Vivian __ _____ before _____.

重點結構：before 的用法

解　答：<u>Vivian studied for three hours before she went out to get some sunshine.</u>

或　　<u>Vivian studied for three hours before going out to get some sunshine.</u>

句型分析：主詞 + 動詞 + before + 主詞 + 動詞

或　　主詞 + 動詞 + before + 動名詞

說　明：then「然後」表示薇薇安先念三個小時的書，再外出曬太陽，現在用 before「在～之前」來表示事情的先後順序。而 before 有兩種詞性，若作為連接詞，引導副詞子句時，須接完整的主詞與動詞，即 before she went out to get some sunshine；若作為介系詞，後面須接名詞或動名詞，即 before going out to get some sunshine。

* *go out* 外出　　sunshine〔'sʌn,ʃaɪn〕 *n.* 陽光

10. I want to see the scary movie.
My friend doesn't want to see the scary movie.
I ＿＿＿＿＿＿＿ the scary movie, ＿＿＿＿＿＿＿＿＿ it.

重點結構：but 的用法

解　答：<u>I want to see the scary movie, but my friend doesn't want to see it.</u>

句型分析：主詞 + 動詞 + but + 主詞 + 動詞

說　明：but 是對等連接詞，表示語氣上的轉折。

* *scary movie* 恐怖片（= *horror movie*）

第 11～15 題：重組

11. Chris _____.

since / interested in / has / English / he / been / child / was / a

　　重點結構：since 的用法

　　　解　答：<u>Chris has been interested in English since he</u>
　　　　　　　<u>was a child.</u>

　　句型分析：主詞＋動詞＋since＋主詞＋動詞

　　　説　明：連接詞 since 引導的副詞子句中，動詞時態用過
　　　　　　　去式，主要子句中的動詞時態則須用現在完成式，
　　　　　　　表示「從過去繼續到現在的狀態」。

　　* **be interested in** 對～有興趣　　since〔sɪns〕*conj.* 自從

12. Winnie _____.

such / have / feels / strict / lucky / to / a / teacher / so

　　重點結構：so 與 such 的用法

　　　解　答：<u>Winnie feels so lucky to have such a strict</u>
　　　　　　　<u>teacher.</u>

　　句型分析：主詞＋動詞＋so＋形容詞＋to have＋such＋名詞

　　　説　明：so 和 such 都作「如此」解，但 so 是副詞，修飾
　　　　　　　形容詞 lucky，such 則是形容詞，修飾名詞片語
　　　　　　　a strict teacher。

　　* lucky〔ˈlʌkɪ〕*adj.* 幸運的　　strict〔strɪkt〕*adj.* 嚴格的

13. George _____.

the ceiling / too / reach / short / is / to

重點結構：「too…to V.」的用法

　解　答：George is too short to reach the ceiling.

句型分析：主詞 + be 動詞 + too + 形容詞 + to V.

　說　明：這題的意思是說「喬治太矮了，用手碰不到天花
　　　　　　板」，用 too…to V. 合併，表「太…以致於不～」。

* reach〔ritʃ〕v. 用手碰到　　ceiling〔'silɪŋ〕n. 天花板

14. The _____.

writing / policeman / a / is / parking ticket

重點結構：現在進行式字序

　解　答：The policeman is writing a parking ticket.

句型分析：主詞 + be 動詞 + 現在分詞

　說　明：這題的意思是說「警察正在開違規停車的罰單」，
　　　　　　is writing 為現在進行式，即「be 動詞 + 現在分詞」
　　　　　　的形式。

* policeman〔pə'lismən〕n. 警察
　parking ticket 違規停車的罰單

15. Teresa _____.

take out / her father / forgot / the / to / for / garbage

重點結構：forget 的用法

　解　答：Teresa forgot to take out the garbage for her
　　　　　father.

句型分析：主詞 + forget + to V.

　說　明：「忘記去做某件事」用 forget + to V. 來表示，此
　　　　　　題須在 forgot（forget 的過去式）後面接不定詞。

* *take out* 拿出去　　garbage〔'gɑrbɪdʒ〕n. 垃圾

第二部份：段落寫作

題目：今天你運氣不好，碰到一連串不如意的事。請根據以下的圖
片寫一篇約 50 字的短文。

I had a bad day today. I woke up at nine o'clock. I was late for school and my teacher was angry. *Then* I dropped my glasses. They broke. I took a bus home. *But* I left my wallet on the bus. When I got home, I could not open the door because I did not have my key. *What a terrible day!*

我今天運氣不好。我九點起床。我上學遲到，老師很生氣。然後，我眼鏡掉了。它們破掉了。我搭公車回家。但次我把皮夾遺留在公車上。當我到家的時候，我無法打開門，因為我沒有鑰匙。真是糟糕的一天！

have a bad day 那天運氣不好　　***wake up*** 醒來
angry〔'æŋgrı〕*adj.* 生氣的　　drop〔drɑp〕*v.* 掉落
glasses〔'glæsɪz〕*n. pl.* 眼鏡　　break〔brek〕*v.* 破碎
leave〔liv〕*v.* 遺留　　wallet〔'wɑlɪt〕*n.* 錢包
key〔ki〕*n.* 鑰匙

口說能力測驗詳解

*請在 15 秒內完成並唸出下列自我介紹的句子：

My seat number is （複試座位號碼後 5 碼）, and my test number is （初試准考證號碼後 5 碼）.

I. 複誦

共五題。題目不印在試卷上，由耳機播出，
每題播出兩次，兩次之間大約有一至二秒
的間隔。聽完兩次後，請馬上複誦一次。

1. Give me a second. 給我一點時間。

2. Are these boxes big enough? 這些箱子夠大嗎？

3. Who is painting the bathroom? 誰在粉刷浴室？

4. Slow down. You walk too fast.
   慢一點。你走太快了。

5. Is Mom and Dad's anniversary on Saturday or Sunday?
   爸媽的結婚週年是在週六還是週日？

【註】 second〔ˈsɛkənd〕n. 秒；一會兒　　box〔bɑks〕n. 箱子
enough〔ɪˈnʌf〕adj. 足夠的　　paint〔pet〕v. 粉刷；油漆
bathroom〔ˈbæθˌrum〕n. 浴室　　**slow down** 慢下來
walk〔wɔk〕v. 走
anniversary〔ˌænɪˈvɝsərɪ〕n. 週年紀念

II. 朗讀句子與短文

共有五個句子及一篇短文,請先利用一分
鐘的時間閱讀試卷上的句子與短文,然後
在一分鐘內以正常的速度,清楚正確的朗讀一遍,閱讀時請不要
發出聲音。

One　: Jack fixed his computer and painted his living room
　　　today.
　　　傑克今天修理他的電腦並粉刷客廳。

Two　: Laura's mother taught her how to bake cookies.
　　　蘿拉的母親教她如何烤餅乾。

Three : My father has a friend who speaks nine languages
　　　fluently.
　　　我父親有一位能流利地說九種語言的朋友。

Four　: It took me several weeks to finish reading the book,
　　　but I finally did it.
　　　我花了好幾週才讀完這本書,但是我最後做到了。

Five　: The library will be open during the holidays.
　　　圖書館假日會開放。

【註】 fix〔fɪks〕v. 修理　　　***living room*** 客廳
　　　taught〔tɔt〕v. 教導【teach 的過去式】
　　　bake〔kek〕v. 烤;烘焙　　cookie〔'kʊkɪ〕n. 餅乾
　　　language〔'læŋgwɪdʒ〕n. 語言

fluently〔'fluəntlɪ〕*adv.* 流利地
several〔'sɛvərəl〕*adj.* 好幾個的
finally〔'faɪnlɪ〕*adv.* 最後
library〔'laɪˌbrɛrɪ〕*n.* 圖書館
open〔'opən〕*adj.* 開放的
during〔'djʊrɪŋ〕*prep.* 在…的期間

Six ： Recently our science class went on a field trip. It was very interesting and lots of fun. We went to a forest to look at trees and plants. Our teacher, Mr. Liu, told us to write down everything we saw in our notebooks.

最近我們自然課去校外教學。這非常有趣又好玩。我們去森林裡看樹和植物。我們的老師，劉老師，告訴我們要把看到的東西記錄在筆記本上。

【註】 recently〔'risn̩tlɪ〕*adv.* 最近
science〔'saɪəns〕*n.* 科學；自然　　*go on a trip* 去旅行
field trip 校外教學　　interesting〔'ɪntərɪstɪŋ〕*adj.* 有趣的
forest〔'fɔrɪst〕*n.* 森林　　plant〔plænt〕*n.* 植物
Mr.〔'mɪstɚ〕*n.* …先生；…老師
told〔told〕*v.* 告訴【tell 的過去式】
write down 寫下；記下
saw〔sɔ〕*v.* 看到【see 的過去式】
notebook〔'notˌbʊk〕*n.* 筆記本

Ⅲ. 回答問題

共七題。題目不印在試卷上，由耳機播出，
每題播出兩次，兩次之間大約有一至二秒的
間隔。聽完兩次後，請馬上回答。每題回答時間為 15 秒，回答
時不一定要用完整的句子，請在作答時間內儘量的表達。

1. **Q**：What time did you get here today? Did you have time
　　to look around?
　　你今天幾點到這裡的？你有時間四處看看嗎？

　　A：I got here at 7:45. I had 15 minutes to get ready, but I
　　didn't really look around. 我七點四十五分到這的。我有
　　十五分鐘準備，但是我沒能真的四處看看。

　　【註】*look around* 四處看看；參觀

2. **Q**：Will you be busy next week? Why or why not?
　　你下週會很忙嗎？為何或為何不？

　　A：Yes, I will be busy next week. I have several big
　　exams coming up.
　　是的，我下週會很忙。我有幾個重要的考試要考。

　　【註】busy〔'bIzI〕*adj.* 忙碌的　　big〔bIg〕*adj.* 重要的
　　　　exam〔Ig'zæm〕*n.* 考試　　*come up* 發生；即將到來

3. **Q**：What's the weather like during a typhoon?
　　颱風來的時候天氣如何？

　　A：During a typhoon, there are strong winds and heavy
　　rain. 颱風來的時候，有強風跟大雨。

　　【註】weather〔'wɛðɚ〕*n.* 天氣　　typhoon〔taI'fun〕*n.* 颱風
　　　　strong〔strɔŋ〕*adj.* 強力的　　wind〔wInd〕*n.* 風
　　　　heavy rain 大雨

4. **Q**：What's your favorite meal of the day? Describe what
you normally eat.

你一天最喜愛的餐點是什麼？描述一下你通常吃的東西。

A：Lunch is my favorite meal of the day. I usually have
a vegetarian meal from the cafeteria downstairs. So I
usually eat vegetables and rice.

午餐是我一天最喜歡的一餐。我通常吃樓下自助餐廳的
素食。所有我一般都吃蔬菜和米飯。

【註】 favorite〔'fevərɪt〕*adj.* 最喜愛的
meal〔mil〕*n.* 一餐　　describe〔dɪ'skraɪb〕*v.* 描述
normally〔'nɔrml̩ɪ〕*adv.* 正常地；通常
usually〔'juʒʊəlɪ〕*adv.* 通常；一般
vegetarian〔,vɛdʒə'tɛrɪən〕*adj.* 速食的
cafeteria〔,kæfə'tɪrɪə〕*n.* 自助餐廳
downstairs〔'daʊn'stɛrz〕*adv.* 在樓下
vegetables〔'vɛdʒətəbl̩z〕*n. pl.* 蔬菜　　rice〔raɪs〕*n.* 米

5. **Q**：How does one go about caring for a pet?

一個人要如何著手照顧寵物？

A：Well, you have to feed it and make sure it gets enough
exercise. You also have to make sure it's safe, so you
can't let it run free. Mostly, I think you just have to
love your pet.　嗯，你必須餵牠，並且確定牠有足夠的運
動。你也必須確定牠夠安全，所以你不能讓牠隨處走動。
基本上，我覺得你就是得愛你的寵物。

【註】 *go about* 處理；著手　　*care for* 照顧
pet〔pɛt〕*n.* 寵物　　well〔wɛl〕*interj.* 嗯
have to V. 必須～　　feed〔fid〕*v.* 餵
make sure 確認　　exercise〔'ɛksə,saɪz〕*n.* 運動
safe〔sef〕*adj.* 安全的　　*run free* 自由奔跑；隨處走動
mostly〔'mostlɪ〕*adv.* 大半；主要地；基本上

6. **Q**：Have you ever traveled abroad? Tell me about your trip. If you haven't, tell me where you'd like to visit most. 你曾經去出國旅遊嗎？告訴我關於你旅行的事。如果你沒有過，告訴我你最想要去哪。

A：I have never traveled abroad. But I would like to visit Canada and Australia the most.

我從來沒有出國旅行過。但是我最想要去加拿大跟澳洲。

【註】 travel〔'trævl〕*v.* 旅行

abroad〔ə'brɔd〕*adv.* 國外；海外　　trip〔trɪp〕*n.* 旅行

would like to V. 想要～　　visit〔'vɪzɪt〕*v.* 參觀；探訪

Canada〔'kænədə〕*n.* 加拿大

Australia〔ɔ'streljə〕*n.* 澳洲

7. **Q**：Your friend Fred isn't feeling very well today. What could you say to him?

你的朋友弗瑞德今天感到不太舒服。你可以對他說什麼？

A：Not feeling well today, Fred? What's wrong? Have you taken any medication? Maybe you need some rest. Why don't you go home and get better?

今天覺得不舒服嗎，弗雷德？怎麼了？你吃藥了嗎？或許你需要休息一下。你何不回家讓身體復原？

【註】 feel〔fil〕*v.* 感覺；感到

well〔wɛl〕*adj.* 健康的；舒服的

medication〔ˌmɛdɪ'keʃən〕*n.* 藥物　　rest〔rɛst〕*n.* 休息

why don't you V. 你何不～（＝ *why not* ）

get better 情況變好；復原

* 請將下列自我介紹的句子再唸一遍：

My seat number is （複試座位號碼後 5 碼） , and my test number is （初試准考證號碼後 5 碼）.

初級英語檢定複試測驗⑪詳解

寫作能力測驗詳解

第一部份：單句寫作

第 1~5 題：句子改寫

1. I asked Amy, "Could you pass me some napkins?"
   I asked Amy if _____ pass me some napkins.

   重點結構：直接問句改為間接問句的用法

   解　答：<u>I asked Amy if she could pass me some napkins.</u>

   句型分析：I asked Amy + if + 主詞 + 動詞

   說　明：Could you pass me some napkins? 是直接問句，
   現在要放在 if（是否）後面，做為 I asked Amy 的
   受詞，即名詞子句（間接問句）「連接詞 + 主詞 +
   動詞」的形式，在 I asked Amy 後面接 if she could
   pass me some napkins，並把問號改成句點。

   * pass〔pæs〕v. 傳遞　　napkin〔'næpkɪn〕n. 餐巾紙

2. Helen seldom rides a bike home.
   _____ last month.

   重點結構：過去式動詞

   解　答：<u>Helen seldom rode a bike home last month.</u>

   句型分析：主詞 + 動詞 + 時間副詞

   說　明：時間副詞為 last month，故動詞要改為過去式，
   rides 改成 rode。

* seldom〔'sɛldəm〕*adv.* 很少
  bike〔baɪk〕*n.* 腳踏車

3. Lisa and her cousin played table tennis.

   When _____?

   重點結構：wh- 問句的用法

   　解　答：<u>When did Lisa and her cousin play table tennis?</u>

   句型分析：When + 助動詞 + 主詞 + 動詞？

   　說　明：played 為過去式動詞，故助動詞用 did，主詞後的
   　　　　　動詞須用原形動詞 play。

   * cousin〔'kʌzn̩〕*n.* 堂（表）兄弟姊妹　　***table tennis*** 桌球

4. John：Did you go to the library to return my books?

   Nick：Oh, I forgot.

   Nick forgot _____ to return John's books.

   重點結構：「forget + to V.」的用法

   　解　答：<u>Nick forgot to go to the library to return John's</u>
   　　　　　<u>books.</u>

   句型分析：主詞 + forget + to V.

   　說　明：「忘記去做某件事」用 forget + to V. 來表示，
   　　　　　此題須在 forgot 後面接不定詞。

   * library〔'laɪ,brɛrɪ〕*n.* 圖書館　　return〔rɪ'tɜn〕*v.* 歸還

5. To go traveling in Africa is my dream.

   It's _____.

重點結構：以 It 爲虛主詞引導的句子

解　答：<u>It's my dream to go traveling in Africa.</u>

句型分析：It's + 形容詞 + to V.

説　明：虛主詞 It 代替不定詞片語，眞正的主詞是不定詞

　　　　片語 to go traveling in Africa，放在句尾。

＊ **go traveling**　去旅行　　Africa〔'æfrɪkə〕*n.* 非洲

　dream〔drim〕*n.* 夢想

第 6～10 題：句子合併

6. Laura asked Linda something.

   The computer didn't work.

   Laura asked Linda why ＿＿＿＿＿＿＿＿＿＿＿＿＿＿＿＿.

重點結構：名詞子句當受詞用

解　答：<u>Laura asked Linda why the computer didn't work.</u>

句型分析：Laura asked Linda + why + 主詞 + 動詞

説　明：題目中，蘿拉要問琳達一件事，就是關於電腦不能

　　　　用這件事，兩句之間用疑問詞 why 來合併，如果是

　　　　直接問句的話，我們會說："Why didn't /doesn't

　　　　the computer work?"，但這裡前面有 Laura asked

　　　　Linda，因此後面必須接名詞子句，做爲受詞，即

　　　　「疑問詞 + 主詞 + 動詞」的形式，在 Laura asked

　　　　Linda 後面接 why the computer didn't work。

＊ computer〔kəm'pjutɚ〕*n.* 電腦

　work〔wɝk〕*v.*（機器）運轉

7. You can play video games.

   You finish your homework.

   You _____ as long as _____.

> 重點結構：as long as 的用法
>
> 解　答：You can play video games as long as you finish your homework.
>
> 句型分析：主詞 + 動詞 + as long as + 主詞 + 動詞
>
> 說　明：這題的句意是「你可以打電動玩具，只要你把功課做完。」as long as「只要」為連接詞片語，故後面要接完整的子句，即主詞加動詞的形式。
>
> * **video game** 電動玩具　　**as long as** 只要

8. Patricia takes a shower.

   Then she has dinner.

   Patricia _____ after _____.

> 重點結構：after 的用法
>
> 解　答：Patricia has dinner after she takes a shower.
>
> 或　　　Patricia has dinner after (taking) a shower.
>
> 句型分析：主詞 + 動詞 + before + 主詞 + 動詞
>
> 或　　　主詞 + 動詞 + before + （動）名詞
>
> 說　明：then「然後」表示派翠西亞先洗澡，再吃晚餐，現在用 after「在～之後」來表示事情的先後順序。而 after 有兩種詞性，若作為連接詞，引導副詞子句時，須接完整的主詞與動詞，即 after she takes a shower；若作為介系詞，後面須接名詞或動名詞，即 after a shower 或 after taking a shower。

＊ ***take a shower*** 淋浴　　have〔hæv〕v. 吃

9. Gail cleans the classroom.

David helps her.

David helps Gail _____.

　重點結構：「help + *sb*. + (to) V.」的用法

　解　答：David helps Gail (to) clean the classroom.

　句型分析：help + 受詞 + 不定詞或原形動詞

　說　明：這題句意是「大衛幫蓋兒打掃教室」，help 的用法
　　　　　是接受詞後，須接不定詞，不定詞的 to 也可省略。

　＊ clean〔klin〕v. 打掃

10. I will go to the supermarket tomorrow.

I'll mail the letter for you.

I'll mail the letter for you when _____ tomorrow.

　重點結構：未來式的 wh- 問句

　解　答：I'll mail the letter for you when I go to the
　　　　　supermarket tomorrow.

　句型分析：I'll mail the letter for you + when + 主詞 + 動詞

　說　明：在表時間的副詞子句中，要用現在式代替未來式，
　　　　　所以雖然「我明天將去超級市場」是未來的時間，
　　　　　但不能造 when I *will go* to the supermarket
　　　　　tomorrow，須用 when I *go* to the supermarket
　　　　　tomorrow。

　＊ supermarket〔'supɚ͵mɑrkɪt〕n. 超級市場
　　mail〔mel〕v. 郵寄　　letter〔'lɛtɚ〕n. 信

第 11～15 題：重組

11. How many ＿＿＿＿＿＿＿＿＿＿＿＿＿＿＿＿＿＿＿＿＿？

　　does / have / grandchildren / Vincent

　　　重點結構：「How many + 複數名詞？」的用法

　　　　解　答：<u>How many grandchildren does Vincent have?</u>

　　　句型分析：How many + 複數名詞 + 助動詞 + 主詞 + 動詞

　　　　説　明：「How many + 複數名詞？」表「～有（多
　　　　　　　　　少）？」。

　　　＊ grandchildren〔'grænd,tʃɪldrən〕*n. pl.* 孫子（女）

12. My ＿＿＿＿＿＿＿＿＿＿＿＿＿＿＿＿＿＿＿＿＿．

　　goes / work / MRT / usually / by / to / father

　　　重點結構：usually 的用法

　　　　解　答：<u>My father usually goes to work by MRT.</u>

　　　句型分析：主詞 + usually + 一般動詞

　　　　説　明：usually 為頻率副詞，須置於一般動詞的前面。
　　　　　　　　　而「by + 交通工具」表「搭乘～」，置於句尾。

13. Swimming ＿＿＿＿＿＿＿＿＿＿＿＿＿＿＿＿＿＿＿＿．

　　one / is / favorite / sports / my / of

　　　重點結構：「one of + 所有格 + 複數名詞」的用法

　　　　解　答：<u>Swimming is one of my favorite sports.</u>

　　　句型分析：主詞 + be 動詞 + one of + 所有格 + 複數名詞

　　　　説　明：本題是說「游泳是我最喜愛的運動之一」，

　　「～當中的一個」用「one of + 複數名詞」
　　來表示。

14. Mr. Kelly _____.

worked / has / for / in / years / elementary school / the / three

　重點結構：現在完成式字序

　　解　答：Mr. Kelly has worked in the elementary school
　　　　　　for three years.

　句型分析：主詞 + have/has + 過去分詞 + for + 一段時間

　　說　明：現在完成式的結構是「主詞 + have/has + 過去
　　　　　　　分詞」，而「for + 一段時間」，表「持續（多
　　　　　　　久）」，此時間片語須置於句尾。

　＊ *elementary school* 小學

15. This _____.

most / have / building / I / is / beautiful / the / ever / seen

　重點結構：形容詞最高級的用法

　　解　答：This is the most beautiful building I have ever
　　　　　　seen.

　句型分析：the most + 形容詞

　　說　明：beautiful 為兩個音節以上的形容詞，故前面加
　　　　　　most，形成最高級。I have ever seen 作形容詞
　　　　　　子句，修飾 building。

　＊ building〔ˈbɪldɪŋ〕 *n.* 建築物

第二部份：段落寫作

題目：昨天媽媽過生日，你和弟弟一起去買禮物，最後挑了一支手
　　　錶送給媽媽。請根據以下的圖片寫一篇約 50 字的短文。

Yesterday was my mother's birthday. My brother and
I went to a department store to buy a gift. We wanted to
buy some beautiful clothes, but we did not see anything we
liked. *In the end*, we bought her a new watch. It is very
fashionable. *Last night* we had a birthday party. We sang
and ate cake. We also gave our mother the present. She
was very happy.

昨天是我媽媽的生日。我弟弟和我去一家百貨公司買禮物。我
們想要買一些漂亮的衣服，但是我們沒有看到任何我們喜歡的東
西。最後，我們買給她一支新的手錶。這錶非常的時髦。昨晚我們
舉辦生日派對。我們唱歌和吃蛋糕。我們也送給母親禮物。她非常
高興。

> *department store* 百貨公司
> gift〔gɪft〕*n.* 禮物（= *present*）　　*in the end* 最後
> fashionable〔'fæʃənəbl̩〕*adj.* 流行的；時髦的
> *have a birthday party* 舉行生日派對
> present〔'prɛznt〕*n.* 禮物

口說能力測驗詳解

＊請在15秒內完成並唸出下列自我介紹的句子：

My seat number is (複試座位號碼後5碼) , and my test
number is (初試准考證號碼後5碼) .

I. 複誦

共五題。題目不印在試卷上，由耳機播出，
每題播出兩次，兩次之間大約有一至二秒
的間隔。聽完兩次後，請馬上複誦一次。

1. That's a huge fish! 那是一條大魚！

2. I'm going home now. 我現在要回家。

3. Do you hear that noise?
   你有聽到那噪音嗎？

4. I think my cat needs to go on a diet.
   我覺得我的貓需要節食。

5. He failed all his exams.
   他考試全部都不及格。

【註】huge〔hjudʒ〕*adj.* 巨大的　　fish〔fɪʃ〕*n.* 魚
　　　noise〔nɔɪz〕*n.* 噪音　　***go on a diet*** 節食
　　　fail〔fel〕*v.* 考不及格

II. 朗讀句子與短文

共有五個句子及一篇短文，請先利用一分
鐘的時間閱讀試卷上的句子與短文，然後

在一分鐘內以正常的速度，清楚正確的朗讀一遍，閱讀時請不要
發出聲音。

One : Steve was doing his homework on the computer
when the power suddenly went out.
史蒂夫在電腦上做功課，這時突然斷電。

Two : That coffee shop opened shortly after Chinese New
Year.
那家咖啡店在中國農曆新年過後不久開業。

Three : Don't worry about the test tomorrow. I'm sure
you'll do fine.
不要擔心明天的考試。我確定你會考得好。

Four : Mike was so bored that he fell asleep during the
lecture and was scolded by the professor.
麥可覺得很無聊以致於他在講課的時候睡著，而被教授
責罵。

Five : The report is due in less than an hour.
這報告一小時內要交。

【註】power〔ˋpaʊɚ〕 n. 電力　suddenly〔ˋsʌdn̩lɪ〕 adv. 突然
go out 熄滅　***coffee shop*** 咖啡店

shortly〔'tʃɔrtlɪ〕adv. 不久；很快
fine〔faɪn〕adv. 很好地　　lecture〔'lɛktʃə〕n. 講課
scold〔skold〕v. 責備　　professor〔prə'fɛsə〕n. 教授
due〔dju〕adj. 到期的

Six　：Dave likes to eat at the "all you can eat" hotpot
　　　restaurant on Heping East Road. He gets two hours
　　　to eat as much as he can stuff into his face. When
　　　he leaves the restaurant, he's so full he can barely
　　　walk. However, he always has room for ice cream.

　　　戴夫喜歡去和平東路的「吃到飽」火鍋餐廳吃飯。他盡可
　　　能在兩個小時內把食物塞進嘴裡。當他離開餐廳時，他吃
　　　得如此的飽，而幾乎無法走路。不過，他的肚子總是有空
　　　間可以吃冰淇淋。

【註】*all you can eat* 吃到飽；自助餐
　　　hotpot〔'hatpat〕n. 火鍋　　stuff〔stʌf〕v. 裝進；填飽
　　　clothing〔'kloðɪŋ〕n. 衣物　　layer〔'leə〕n. 一層
　　　full〔fʊl〕adj. 飽的　　barely〔'bɛrlɪ〕adv. 幾乎不
　　　however〔haʊ'ɛvə〕adv. 不過；然而
　　　room〔rum〕n. 空間　　*ice cream* 冰淇淋

III. 回答問題

共七題。題目不印在試卷上，由耳機播出，
每題播出兩次，兩次之間大約有一至二秒的
間隔。聽完兩次後，請馬上回答。每題回答時間為 15 秒，回答
時不一定要用完整的句子，請在作答時間內儘量的表達。

1. **Q** : How often do you visit temples? 你多久去一次寺廟？

   A : I rarely if ever visit temples, but I do visit my family's
   tomb on Tomb Sweeping Day. 我很少去寺廟，但是我
   的確會在清明節時去看我家人的墳墓。

   【註】 ***how often*** 多常；多久一次
   visit〔'vɪzɪt〕*v.* 參觀；探訪　　temple〔'tɛmpl̩〕*n.* 廟
   rarely〔'rɛrlɪ〕*adv.* 罕見地
   rarely if ever 就算有也很少　　***do + V.*** 真的～；的確～
   tomb〔tum〕*n.* 墳墓
   Tomb Sweeping Day 掃墓節；清明節

2. **Q** : Do you enjoy bicycling? Why or why not?
   你喜歡騎腳踏車嗎？為何或為何不？

   A : I don't really enjoy riding a bicycle. There are too
   many people out on the streets and it's dangerous.
   I'd rather walk. 我不是很喜歡騎腳踏車。有太多人在路
   上，而且很危險。我寧可走路。

   【註】 enjoy〔ɪn'dʒɔɪ〕*v.* 喜歡
   bicycle〔'baɪˌsɪkl̩〕*v.* 騎腳踏車
   dangerous〔'dendʒərəs〕*adj.* 危險的
   would rather + V. 寧可～；寧願～

3. **Q**：What's your ideal vacation?　Tell me about it.
　　你理想的假期是怎樣？告訴我。

　　A：My ideal vacation takes place at the beach.　I enjoy
　　　　relaxing in the warm weather, just taking it easy.
　　　　我理想的假期是在海邊。我喜歡在溫暖的天氣放鬆自己，
　　　　就是輕鬆自在。
　　【註】ideal〔aɪ'diəl〕*adj.* 理想的
　　　　　vacation〔ve'keʃən〕*n.* 假期　　***take place*** 發生
　　　　　relax〔rɪ'læks〕*v.* 放鬆　　weather〔'wɛðɚ〕*n.* 天氣
　　　　　take it easy 放輕鬆

4. **Q**：Have you ever moved before?　How long have you
　　　　lived in your current home?
　　你搬過家嗎？你在你目前的家住了多久？

　　A：I have never moved before.　I have lived in my house
　　　　for 12 years.　我從未搬過家。我住在我家 12 年了。
　　【註】move〔muv〕*v.* 搬家　　current〔'kɝənt〕*adj.* 目前的

5. **Q**：Who's your best friend?　How long have you known
　　　　each other?　你最好的朋友是誰？你們認識彼此多久了？

　　A：My best friend is named Veronica.　We've known
　　　　each other since first grade.
　　　　我最好的朋友叫維羅妮卡。我們從一年級就認識了。
　　【註】***each other*** 彼此　　name〔nem〕*v.* 命名
　　　　　grade〔gred〕*n.* 年級

6. **Q**：What are your friends like? Tell me about them.
   你的朋友如何？告訴我關於他們的事。

   A：My friends are all very athletic. They enjoy all sorts
   of sports and they're very active. They are always up
   for a game, no matter what it is.
   我的朋友們都很會運動。他們喜歡各種的運動，而且他們
   很活潑。他們總是準備好要比賽，不管是什麼樣的。

   【註】athletic〔æθ′lɛtɪk〕*adj.* 運動的
   　　　sort〔sɔrt〕*n.* 種類　　sport〔spɔrt〕*n.* 運動
   　　　active〔′æktɪv〕*adj.* 活潑的；敏捷的
   　　　be up for 準備好　　game〔gem〕*n.* 比賽

7. **Q**：Your friend Bill just heard that his grandmother
   passed away. What could you say to him?
   你的朋友比爾剛聽到他的祖母過世。你能對他說什麼？

   A：I'm sorry for your loss, Bill. Your grandma is in a
   better place now. She's at peace. I'm here for you
   if you need a shoulder to cry on.
   比爾，我對你喪失親人感到難過。你祖母現在在更美好的地
   方。她安息了。我在這等你，如果你需要傾訴的話。

   【註】grandmother〔′græn,mʌðɚ〕*n.* 祖母（ = *grandma*）
   　　　pass away 去世　　loss〔lɔs〕*n.* 喪失
   　　　at peace 安息；去世（ = *dead*）
   　　　a shoulder to cry on 能提供慰藉的人；可以傾訴的對象

＊請將下列自我介紹的句子再唸一遍：

My seat number is 　(複試座位號碼後 5 碼)　, and my test

number is 　(初試准考證號碼後 5 碼)　.

初級英語檢定複試測驗⑫詳解

寫作能力測驗詳解

第一部份：單句寫作

第 1~5 題：句子改寫

1. She wrote this famous novel.

   This famous novel ＿＿＿＿＿＿＿＿＿＿＿＿＿＿＿ her.

   　重點結構：被動語態字序

   　　解　答：<u>This famous novel was written by her.</u>

   　句型分析：主詞 + be 動詞 + 過去分詞 + by + 受詞

   　　説　明：被動語態的形式是「be 動詞 + 過去分詞」，

   　　　　　　故動詞 wrote 須改爲 was written。

   　* famous〔ˊfeməs〕adj. 有名的　　novel〔ˊnɑvḷ〕n. 小說

2. Listening to popular music is fun.

   It's ＿＿＿＿＿＿＿＿＿＿＿＿＿＿＿＿＿＿＿.

   　重點結構：以 It 爲虛主詞引導的句子

   　　解　答：<u>It's fun to listen to popular music.</u>

   　句型分析：It's + 形容詞 + to V.

   　　説　明：虛主詞 It 代替不定詞片語，不定詞片語則擺在

   　　　　　　句尾，故 Listening to popular music 改爲 to

   　　　　　　listen to popular music。

* ***listen to*** 聽　　popular〔ˈpɑpjələ〕*adj.* 流行的

fun〔fʌn〕*adj.* 有趣的

3. When will the next bus come?

I'd like to know when _____.

重點結構：間接問句做名詞子句

解　答：<u>I'd like to know when the next bus will come.</u>

句型分析：I'd like to know + when + 主詞 + 動詞

說　明：在 wh- 問句前加 I'd like to know，形成名詞子

句（間接問句），即「疑問詞 + 主詞 + 動詞」的

形式，把 will come 放在最後面，並把問號改成

句點。

4. Nicolas went home after school.

Where _____ after school?

重點結構：過去式的 wh-問句

解　答：<u>Where did Nicolas go after school?</u>

句型分析：Where + did + 主詞 + 原形動詞？

說　明：這一題應將過去式直述句改為 wh-問句，除了要加

助動詞 did，還要記得助動詞後面的動詞，須用原

形動詞，因此 went 要改成 go。

5. My friend gave me a stuffed doll.

My friend _____ me.

重點結構：give 的用法

解　答：<u>My friend gave a stuffed doll to me.</u>

句型分析：give + 直接受詞（物）+ to + 間接受詞（人）

說　明：「把東西給某人」有兩種寫法：

「give + *sb.* + *sth.*」或「give + *sth.* + to + *sb.*」。

這題要改成第二種用法，先寫物（a stuffed

doll），再寫人（me）。

* stuffed〔stʌft〕*adj.* 填充（玩具）的

doll〔dɑl〕*n.* 洋娃娃

第 6～10 題：句子合併

6. Don't drink too much coffee.

You will not fall asleep easily.

Don't drink too much coffee, ＿＿＿＿＿＿＿＿＿＿＿＿＿＿＿＿.

重點結構：祈使句表達條件句的用法

解　答：<u>Don't drink too much coffee, or you will not</u>
<u>fall asleep easily.</u>

句型分析：原形動詞，or + 主詞 + 動詞

說　明：這題的意思是說「不要喝太多咖啡，不然你會不容

易入睡」，連接詞 or 表「否則」。這題可改寫為：

If you drink too much coffee, you will not fall

asleep easily.

* coffee〔'kɔfɪ〕*n.* 咖啡　　***fall asleep*** 睡著

7. We had a music class this morning.

We had a PE class this morning.

We had both a music ＿＿＿＿＿＿＿ this morning.

重點結構：both A and B 的用法

解　答：<u>We had both a music (class) and a PE class</u>
<u>this morning.</u>

句型分析：主詞 + 動詞 + both + 名詞 + and + 名詞

説　明：句意是「我們今天早上，不但有音樂課，還有體育
課」，用「both…and～」合併兩個受詞，表「不
但…而且～」。

* **PE** 體育（ = *physical education* ）

8. The rain is very heavy.

Tammy cannot drive safely.

The rain is too heavy for Tammy ＿＿＿＿＿＿＿＿.

重點結構：「too + 形容詞 + to V.」的用法

解　答：<u>The rain is too heavy for Tammy to drive</u>
<u>safely.</u>

句型分析：主詞 + be 動詞 + too + 形容詞 + to V.

説　明：這題的意思是說「雨太大了，所以泰咪不能安全地
駕駛」，用「too…to V.」合併兩句，表「太…以
致於不～」。

* heavy〔ˋhɛvɪ〕*adj.* 大量的　　safely〔ˋseflɪ〕*adv.* 安全地

9. A cup of coffee costs 50 dollars.

A cup of tea costs 60 dollars.

A cup of tea is _____ than a cup of coffee.

　重點結構：形容詞比較級的用法

　　解　答：<u>A cup of tea is more expensive than a cup of</u>
　　　　　　<u>coffee.</u>

　句型分析：主詞＋be動詞＋比較級形容詞＋than＋受詞

　　說　明：從 than 可看出這是「比較級」的句型，而一杯咖啡
　　　　　　（50元）和一杯茶（60元）的價錢相較之下，茶比
　　　　　　較貴，故用 more expensive，形成比較級。

10. Ron is 18 years old.

He can drive a car.

Ron is old enough _____.

　重點結構：「形容詞＋enough＋to V.」的用法

　　解　答：<u>Ron is old enough to drive a car.</u>

　句型分析：主詞＋be動詞＋形容詞＋enough＋to V.

　　說　明：這題的意思是說「朗年紀夠大，可以開車了」，副
　　　　　　詞 enough「足夠地」須置於要修飾的形容詞之後，
　　　　　　「足以～」則以 enough 加不定詞表示。

第 11～15 題：重組

11. Caroline _____.

couldn't sleep / that / nervous / she / so / was

重點結構：「so + 形容詞 + that 子句」的用法

解　答：<u>Caroline was so nervous that she couldn't sleep.</u>

句型分析：主詞 + be 動詞 + so + 形容詞 + that + 主詞 + 動詞

說　明：這題的意思是說「凱洛琳太緊張了，所以睡不著」，合併兩句時，用「so…that～」，表「如此…以致於～」。

＊ nervous〔'nɝvəs〕*adj.* 緊張的

12. Neither I _____.

can / sister / my / nor / cook

重點結構：「neither…nor～」的用法

解　答：<u>Neither I nor my sister can cook.</u>

句型分析：Neither + A + nor + B + 助動詞 + 動詞

說　明：這題是說我不會說做菜，我姊姊也不會做菜，所以兩個人都不會做菜，用「neither…nor～」來連接兩個主詞，表「兩者皆不」。

＊ cook〔kʊk〕*v.* 煮飯；做菜

13. I asked Mother _____.

at the station / she / pick me up / could / if

重點結構：由連接詞 if 引導的子句

解　答：<u>I asked Mother if she could pick me up at the station.</u>

句型分析：I asked Mother + if + 主詞 + 動詞

說　明：I asked Mother 後面少受詞，現在 if（是否）引導
　　　　名詞子句，做 I asked Mother 的受詞，即名詞子句
　　　　「連接詞＋主詞＋動詞」的形式。

* *pick sb. up* 開車接某人

14. Jenny _____.

Nicolas / a pen / his birthday / sent / for

重點結構：send 的用法

解　答：Jenny sent Nicolas a pen for his birthday.

句型分析：send ＋ 間接受詞（人）＋ 直接受詞（物）

說　明：「寄東西給某人」有兩種寫法：「send ＋ *sb.* ＋ *sth.*」
　　　　或「send ＋ *sth.* ＋ to ＋ *sb.*」，題目中沒有介系詞
　　　　to，所以要採用第一種寫法，先寫人（Nicolas），
　　　　再寫物（a pen），而 for 表「爲了～（原因）」。

15. _____, please?

paper / you / me / another / Could / give

重點結構：Could 開頭問句的用法

解　答：Could you give me another paper, please?

句型分析：Could ＋ 主詞 ＋ 動詞？

說　明：本句是問「可以請你給我另外一張紙嗎？」即問句
　　　　的形式，先寫助動詞 Could，再寫主詞。

第二部份：段落寫作

題目： 昨天你和朋友坐捷運到動物園，看到你最喜歡的動物——
企鵝（penguins）。請根據以下的圖片寫一篇約 50 字的
短文。

Yesterday I went to the zoo with my friend. We took
the MRT. It was very fast. When we got there, there were
many people waiting in line. We bought our tickets and
went inside. We saw many animals in the zoo. I liked them
all, **but** my favorite animals were the penguins. I had a very
good time at the zoo yesterday.

昨天我和我的朋友去動物園。我們坐捷運。一下就到了。當我
們到那，有很多人在排隊。我們買了票入場。我們看到很多動物在
動物園裡面。牠們我全部都喜歡，但是我最喜歡的動物是企鵝。我
昨天在動物園玩得很愉快。

zoo〔zu〕*n.* 動物園
MRT 大眾捷運系統（= *Mass Rapid Transit*）
wait in line 排隊等候　　ticket〔'tɪkɪt〕*n.* 門票
inside〔'ɪn'saɪd〕*adv.* 往裡面　　animal〔'ænəml̩〕*n.* 動物
penguin〔'pɛngwɪn〕*n.* 企鵝　　**have a good time** 玩得愉快

口說能力測驗詳解

*請在 15 秒內完成並唸出下列自我介紹的句子：

My seat number is （複試座位號碼後 5 碼）, and my test number is （初試准考證號碼後 5 碼）.

I. 複誦

共五題。題目不印在試卷上，由耳機播出，每題播出兩次，兩次之間大約有一至二秒的間隔。聽完兩次後，請馬上複誦一次。

1. Have a nice day. 祝你有個美好的一天。

2. Is that a new watch? 那是新的手錶嗎？

3. Looks like it might rain today.
   看起來今天可能會下雨？

4. I wasn't expecting to see you here today.
   我沒想到今天會在這裡看到你。

5. We've been waiting for almost an hour.
   我們等了快要一小時了。

【註】 watch〔watʃ〕n. 手錶　　(it) *looks like* 看起來
rain〔ren〕v. 下雨　　expect〔ɪkˈspɛkt〕v. 預期；期待
wait〔wet〕v. 等待　　almost〔ˈɔlˌmost〕adv. 幾乎；將近

II. 朗讀句子與短文

共有五個句子及一篇短文,請先利用一分
鐘的時間閱讀試卷上的句子與短文,然後
在一分鐘內以正常的速度,清楚正確的朗讀一遍,閱讀時請不要
發出聲音。

One : Don't say that! She might hear you.

不要說!她可能會聽到。

Two : Someone stole my bicycle; luckily, I was planning
to buy a new one this weekend.

某人偷了我的腳踏車;幸好,我計畫這週末要買台新的。

Three : Have you finished washing the dishes yet?

你已經洗好碗了嗎?

Four : Who's taking care of your dog while your family
goes on vacation?

你全家去度假時,誰照顧你的狗?

Five : I told him not to start a fight with Lou, but he didn't
listen.

我告訴他不要和盧爭吵,但他不聽。

【註】 stole〔stol〕v. 偷【steal 的過去式】
bicycle〔'baɪˌsɪkḷ〕n. 腳踏車
luckily〔'lʌkɪlɪ〕adv. 幸運地
plan〔plæn〕v. 計畫;打算

weekend〔'wik'ɛnd〕*n.* 週末

dishes〔'dɪʃɪz〕*n. pl.* 碗盤；餐具

take care of 照顧　***go on vacation*** 去度假

start a fight 挑起爭端；爭吵

Six　：When buying a pair of sunglasses, you should
always try them on first, and stare up into the sun.
Make sure the lenses are dark enough to protect
your eyes from the sunlight.　Then, if possible,
look in a mirror to see how the sunglasses fit.

買一副太陽眼鏡的時候，你應該都要先試戴看看，然後
向著太陽注視。確認鏡片夠暗足以保護你的眼睛不要陽
光的傷害。然後，可能的話，照照鏡子看眼鏡適不適
合。

【註】　pair〔pɛr〕*n.* 一雙

sunglasses〔'sʌnglæsɪz〕*n. pl.* 太陽眼鏡

try on 試戴；試穿　stare〔stɛr〕*v.* 注視；凝視

make sure 確認　lens〔lɛnz〕*n.* 鏡片

dark〔dɑrk〕*adj.* 暗的　***enough to V.*** 足以~

protect〔prə'tɛkt〕*v.* 保護 <*from*>

sunlight〔'sʌn,laɪt〕*n.* 陽光

if possible 如果可能的話

mirror〔'mɪrɚ〕*n.* 鏡子　fit〔fɪt〕*v.* 適合

III. 回答問題

共七題。題目不印在試卷上，由耳機播出，
每題播出兩次，兩次之間大約有一至二秒的
間隔。聽完兩次後，請馬上回答。每題回答時間爲 15 秒，回答
時不一定要用完整的句子，請在作答時間内儘量的表達。

1. **Q**：Where do you do most of your studying?
   你大多在哪裡讀書？

   A：I do most of my studying at home.
   我大多在家裡讀書。
   【註】*do one's V-ing* 做～　　study〔ˋstʌdɪ〕*v.* 讀書

2. **Q**：What are your grades like?
   你的成績如何？

   A：My grades are pretty good.　I could do better, but I'm
   happy with them.
   我的成績很好。我可以更好，但是我已經滿意了。
   【註】grade〔gred〕*n.* 成績　　pretty〔ˋprɪtɪ〕*adv.* 非常
   be happy with 對～高興；對～滿意

3. **Q**：Are you planning to go to college after graduating
   from high school?
   你計畫高中畢業後上大學嗎？

   A：Yes, I am planning to attend college.
   是的，我正打算上大學。

【註】plan〔plæn〕*v.* 計畫；打算　　***go to college*** 上大學

　　　graduate〔'grædʒʊ‚et〕*v.* 畢業

　　　attend〔ə'tɛnd〕*v.* 上（學）

4. **Q** : Who is the oldest living member of your family?
How old are he or she?
你現存家人中最老的成員是誰？他或她幾歲？

A : The oldest living member of my family is my
grandfather. He is 78 years old.
我現存家人中最老的事我祖父。他 78 歲。

【註】living〔'lɪvɪŋ〕*adj.* 活著的

　　　member〔'mɛmbɚ〕*n.* 成員

　　　grandfather〔'græn‚fɑtə〕*n.* 祖父

5. **Q** : Is this test easier or more difficult than you expected?
Please explain.
這考試比你預期中簡單還是難？請解釋。

A : It's neither. I had no expectations coming into this
test. 兩者都不是。我對這考試沒有抱有任何期待。

【註】expect〔ɪk'spɛkt〕*v.* 預期

　　　explain〔ɪk'splen〕*v.* 解釋

　　　expectation〔‚ɛkspɛk'teʃən〕*n.* 期待；預期

　　　come into 捲入

6. **Q** : What can parents do to prevent their child from
spending too much time on the Internet?
父母可以做什麼來阻止他們的孩子花太多時間在網路上？

A : That's a good question. I don't know. Maybe they could take away the kid's smartphone?

那是個好問題。我不知道。或許他們可以拿走孩子的智慧型手機？

【註】 parents〔'pɛrənts〕*n. pl.* 父母
prevent〔prɪ'vɛnt〕*v.* 預防；阻止 <*from*>
Internet〔'ɪntə,nɛt〕*n.* 網際網路
take away 拿走　　kid〔kɪd〕*n.* 小孩
smartphone〔'smɑrt,fon〕*n.* 智慧型手機

7. **Q** : Would you study abroad if you could? Why or why not?

如果可以的話，你會出國唸書嗎？為何或為何不？

A : Of course I would study abroad if I could. It would be a great opportunity to broaden my horizons.

當然，可以的話我會出國唸書。這是個增廣見聞的好機會。

【註】 abroad〔ə'brɔd〕*adv.* 在國外
opportunity〔,ɑpə'tjunətɪ〕*n.* 機會
broaden〔'brɔdn̩〕*v.* 拓寬；增廣
horizons〔hə'raɪznz〕*n. pl.* 知識領域；見識

＊請將下列自我介紹的句子再唸一遍：

My seat number is （複試座位號碼後 5 碼）, and my test number is （初試准考證號碼後 5 碼）.

因為有您，劉毅老師
心存感激，領路教育

　　「領路教育」是2009年成立的一家以英語培訓為主的教育機構，迄今已經發展成為遍佈全國的教育集團。這篇文章講述的是「領路教育」與臺灣教育專家劉毅老師的故事。作為「一口氣英語」的創始人，劉毅老師一直是「領路教育」老師敬仰的楷模。我們希望透過這篇文章，告訴所有教培業同仁，選擇這樣一位導師，選擇「一口氣英語」，會讓你終生受益。

劉毅老師與「領路教育」劉耿董事長合影

一、濟南年會，領路教育派七位老師參加培訓

　　2014年4月，劉毅老師在濟南組織了「第一屆一口氣英語師訓」，這是「一口氣英語」第一次在大陸公開亮相。「領路教育」派出7位老師趕往濟南參加，因為團隊表現優異，榮獲了最優秀團隊獎，Windy老師還獲得了師訓第一名。劉毅老師親自為大家頒發了證書，並且獎勵了Windy老師往返臺灣的機票費用。他希望更多的優秀老師，能夠更快地學到這個方法，造福更多學生。這一期對大陸老師的培訓，推動了兩岸英語教育的交流，也給大陸英語培訓，注入了全新的方式和動力。

二、效果驚人，「領路教育」開辦「一口氣英語班」

　　培訓結束後，「領路教育」很快組織並開設了「暑假一口氣英語演講班」。14天密集上課，孩子們取得的成效令人驚訝！孩子獲得了前所未有的自信！苦練的英文最美，背出的正確英文最自信。孩子們回到學校，走上講臺，脫口而出英文自我介紹時，留給整個課堂的是一片驚訝，和雷鳴般的掌聲！這也讓我們對劉毅「一口氣英語」的教學效果更加信服。

三、Windy老師成為劉毅一口氣英語培訓講師

　　自此，我們開始著手開了更多的「一口氣英語」班級，越來越多的區域出現了非常多優秀的「一口氣英語」老師。「領路教育」逐漸發明了一套「一口氣英語」班級的激勵系統，特色的操練方式和展示的配套動作。由於在「領路教育」有了成功的教學實踐，Windy老師收到劉毅老師的邀請，作為特邀講師，協助「一口氣英語」在各地的師訓工作。

四、連續三場千人講座，助推劉毅一口氣英語的全國傳播

　　2016年10月18日，在「領路人商學院週年慶典暨千人峰會」的同時，「領路教育」順利組織了劉毅「一口氣英語」在長沙的首屆師訓，劉毅老師親臨現場授課，並且接連在長沙、太原、武漢三地開展「劉毅一口氣英語千人講座」，向學生、家長展示「一口氣英語」學習效果，場場爆滿，反應熱烈！